NOL

County Council

Libraries, books and more...........

Please return/renew this item by the last date shown.
Library items may also be renewed by phone on
030 33 33 1234 (24hours) or via our website

www.cumbria.gov.uk/libraries

Cumbria Libraries

CLIC
Interactive Catalogue

Ask for a CLIC password

GOODLY AND GRAVE

In a Bad Case of Kidnap

JUSTINE WINDSOR

ILLUSTRATED BY BECKA MOOR

HarperCollins *Children's Books*

First published in Great Britain by
HarperCollins Children's Books in 2017
HarperCollins Children's Books is a division of HarperCollinsPublishers Ltd,
HarperCollins Publishers
1 London Bridge Street
London SE1 9GF

The HarperCollins website address is:
www.harpercollins.co.uk

1

Text copyright © Justine Windsor 2017
Illustrations copyright © Becka Moor 2017
All rights reserved.

ISBN 978–0–00–818353–0

Justine Windsor and Becka Moor assert the moral right
to be identified as the author and illustrator of the work.

Typeset in Lido 12/18 pt
Printed and bound in England by Clays Ltd, St Ives plc

MIX
Paper from
responsible sources

FSC C007454

FSC™ is a non-profit international organisation established to promote
the responsible management of the world's forests. Products carrying the
FSC label are independently certified to assure consumers that they come
from forests that are managed to meet the social, economic and
ecological needs of present and future generations,
and other controlled sources.

Find out more about HarperCollins and the environment at
www.harpercollins.co.uk/green

For my parents, who read me stories.
And for Charlie, who said I should write my own.

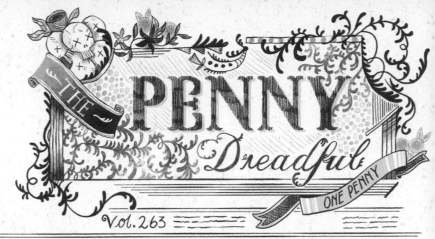

THE **PENNY** *Dreadful*

ONE PENNY

Vol. 263

ANOTHER MISSING CHILD!

THE *PENNY* regrets to inform its readers that another child, Eddie Robinson, went missing several weeks ago. An artist's impression of the child is shown here and a full interview with the unfortunate parents can be found on page two.

ZOMBIES!

On page three, the respected scientist Sir Absalom Balderdash explains how the recent disappearances may be the work of flesh-eating zombies.

CHAPTER ONE

A GAME OF CARDS

idnight in Mrs Milligan's Gambling Den.

Lord Grave puffed on his cigar, blowing smoke into Lucy Goodly's face. She coughed and spluttered and gave Lord Grave her filthiest stare. He'd be less full of himself once she'd relieved him of all the gold in his pockets.

"Finest cigars in the world," Lord Grave said, waving his about.

"You shouldn't smoke in front of me," Lucy said.

"It stunts the growth, you know."

A hush fell over Mrs Milligan's Gambling Den. Dice stopped rolling, roulette wheels stopped turning and everyone held their breath. Lord Grave was the most important customer who'd ever visited Mrs Milligan's. No one else dared complain about his smelly cigar. Lucy's parents, who were sitting at the poker table with Lucy and the eminent Lord, stiffened.

"Fair point," said Lord Grave and stubbed his cigar out on the coat tails of a passing waiter. The waiter bowed, thanked his Lordship and then ran for the kitchens where he sat in a pail of cold water to quench the smouldering embers.

Lord Grave turned back to the Goodlys. "So you've run out of money? No chance of another game?"

"I'm afraid not, your Lordship," said Mrs Goodly. She fiddled with the frayed edge of her shawl, which was more fray than shawl. Lucy's mother had a whole cupboard full of very fine shawls at home, but she always wore her frayed one on poker nights. Lucy herself wore a pair of her father's cut-down breeches and a boy's jacket. And unlike most girls, who favoured curls and ringlets, Lucy liked to keep her straight, shiny black hair short. She found it far more practical.

"Nothing left at all to bet with? Come, now. You must at least have a house?"

"No, sir. We rent a couple of rooms from a Mr Grimes. We share them with three hundred cockroaches, a family of rats and eight slugs. We're very fortunate." Mrs Goodly smiled at Lord Grave in a pathetic way.

Lucy shivered at the idea of sharing a room with three hundred cockroaches, a family of rats and eight slugs. What her mother said wasn't a complete lie. They had once lived in a place like that. But, thanks to Lucy, not any more. Lucy thought of her large, light, clean bedroom in Leafy Ridge, the Goodlys' cottage deep in the country, hundreds of miles away from London and Mrs Milligan's Gambling Den. It was her favourite place in the world. But for the plan to work, the Goodlys had to pretend they still lived in squalor.

"But . . . I do have one thing," said Mrs Goodly,

her voice quivering. Her fingers trembled as she unpinned the brooch fastened lopsidedly to her ragged shawl. It was gold and round, with a red stone in the middle. She placed it on the green cloth of the poker table. Lord Grave picked it up and bit it.

"Real gold? Genuine ruby?"

"Yes, sir. From my dear departed mother, our little Lucy's grandmother."

Lucy put on her best wan smile and patted her mother's hand.

"But . . ." said Mrs Goodly, "Mr Goodly and I, we don't think we have the nerve for another game of poker, sir. Would you consider playing against Lucy instead?"

Lord Grave frowned, his bushy black eyebrows meeting in the middle. He studied Lucy for a few moments. Lucy sat quite still, letting Lord Grave take a good look at her. She knew what he was thinking. That a twelve-year-old girl couldn't possibly beat anyone at poker. But he was wrong. Because Lucy never, ever lost a poker game. Unless she lost on purpose.

"This child?" said Lord Grave eventually. "Not much of a challenge for me!"

"Oh, please, sir," said Mrs Goodly, tears shining in her eyes (beneath the poker table, Lucy was pinching her mother's leg hard in order to make her eyes water). "Otherwise we'll have to sleep in the gutter tonight!"

Lord Grave picked up the ruby brooch and turned it over in his fingers. He nodded. "Very well."

"Oh, thank you, sir!" chorused all three Goodlys.

"One moment." Lord Grave handed the ruby brooch back to Mrs Goodly. "I don't want to play for the brooch. I want to play for the girl."

Lucy's stomach dropped down to her toes. This wasn't how things usually proceeded.

"You want to play for *my daughter*?" said Mr Goodly, running his hand through his untidy dark hair.

"I need a new boot girl for Grave Hall. Little Lucy looks just the ticket. If you win, I'll give you that brooch's value four times over."

"We need time to decide," said Mrs Goodly,

suddenly sounding much less tearful.

"Don't take too long or I may change my mind," said Lord Grave. He got to his feet and strode over to the tiny bar tucked into a corner of the gambling den.

The three Goodlys looked at each other.

"We can't," said Mr Goodly.

"Of course not," Mrs Goodly agreed.

"You know I won't lose," whispered Lucy. "Just think. We'll make enough to live on for years!"

"But you do lose sometimes," said Mr Goodly. "We mustn't risk it!"

Lucy wanted to tell him that she only lost a game now and then so people wouldn't be too suspicious, including her parents. But she couldn't. So she shook her head and said, "Look at him. He's all fuddled with brandy. He's having another glass now." Lord Grave was leaning against the bar, drinking Mrs Milligan's most expensive brandy out of a glass practically the size of Lucy's head.

Mr Goodly took both of Lucy's hands in his. "Dear girl, are you sure?"

"Yes, Father. I won't lose!"

Excitement bubbled up in Lucy. Once she'd beaten Lord Grave, she could spend the rest of the summer paddling and fishing in the river near Leafy Ridge and forget about gambling altogether. And although her parents were hopeless in many ways, she loved them very much and enjoyed spending time with them at home. Her father would bake pies (Lucy picked the scorched pastry off before eating the filling). Her mother would get out her toolbox and crash and bang around inside Leafy Ridge, making improvements (Lucy would then quietly pay someone to improve the improvements). It would be the perfect summer!

Lord Grave staggered back to the table. All of Mrs Milligan's customers trailed after him, whispering behind their hands. Some of them had seen Lucy play poker before and were looking forward to watching her win against this stuck-up man.

"Well?" asked Lord Grave.

"We agree," said Lucy.

"Excellent." Lord Grave clicked his fingers. "A fresh deck of cards, if you please. In fact, let's play with two decks – makes for a more interesting game.

Five-card draw suit you, young lady?"

Lucy nodded.

Mrs Milligan herself pushed her way to the front of the crowd. She had two new packs of cards, which she showed to Lucy and Lord Grave so they could check the seals were intact. Then she shuffled the cards and began to deal.

Lucy's heart thumped with each card that Mrs Milligan flicked down on to the green cloth. *No need to be scared,* she told herself. She touched the right sleeve of her jacket. Tucked up inside was a blank card. The card that had changed her life and that sometimes, when she lay awake in the middle of the night, she feared was the work of the devil. The beautiful woman she'd stolen it from hadn't looked like the devil, though. Apart from the fiery eyes burning behind the veil of her hat.

CHAPTER TWO

JUMPING JACK

When Lucy and Lord Grave both had five cards each, Mrs Milligan placed the rest face down on the table. Then she herded the crowd back.

"Give 'em space," she said. "No funny business."

Lucy picked up her five cards, angling them towards her chest so no one could see what they were.

Four tens and the two of hearts.

The tens were good, but the two might be a disaster.

A king would be so much better. She'd definitely win with a king.

Keeping her gaze fixed steadily on Lord Grave's face, Lucy emptied her mind of everything. The people crowding as close as Mrs Milligan would allow. The smoke stinging her eyes. The smell of brandy and cigars. Even her parents. She pushed them all from her thoughts until the only thing she saw in her imagination was the two of hearts.

Then she imagined the markings on the two of hearts melting, like wax on a candle, sliding off the face of the card and down, down into her sleeve, then reforming on the card hidden there.

When Lucy had finished imagining with all her might, she looked again at the cards she held.

Four tens and one blank card.

She concentrated even harder.

This time she pictured herself holding the king of hearts.

Colours and patterns began swirling across the surface of the blank card. They gathered into the shape of the heads and shoulders of two bearded men, one on the top half of the card, the other upside down at the bottom. Each man wore a golden crown.

Lucy's head began to pound, the start of the headache she always suffered when she performed the trick. Her arms ached, the cards feeling like weights. But the trick had worked. The two of hearts was safely tucked up her sleeve. Now she was holding four tens and the king of hearts.

A winning hand.

"Either of you want to switch?" asked Mrs Milligan, indicating the pile of cards in the middle of the table.

"Not me," Lord Grave replied.

"Nor me," said Lucy.

"You're both ready to call then?" said Mrs Milligan.

Lucy and Lord Grave nodded. Lucy laid out her four tens and her king. At the same time, Lord Grave laid his cards out. Incredibly, he had four tens too, but his fifth card was the jack of hearts.

Kings trump jacks.

Lucy had won!

She was about to leap from her seat and hug her parents. But before she could move, a strange sensation began to seep through her. It was as though ice was crawling up her arms and legs, freezing her in place. The only things she could move were her eyes. Everything around her had frozen too. Mrs Milligan and the rest of the gambling crowd were motionless, their mouths open in mid-shout. Her father's hands were over his face. Her mother's mouth was set in a thin line.

Opposite her, Lord Grave sat staring intently at the cards spread out on the table. Then the strangest thing happened. The heads on the top and bottom of Lord Grave's jack of hearts card moved from side to side, as though checking whether anyone was watching. Then a hand appeared at either side of each of the heads, grabbed the edges of the card and the two jacks pulled themselves up and out of the card, on to the table. Lucy blinked in disbelief as the two figures ran over to Lucy's king of hearts, the tiny spurs on their boots jingling. They helped the two kings step out of Lucy's card. The jacks bowed

to the kings and took their place. Then the two kings marched smartly over to the empty card the jacks had left and climbed into it.

As soon as the kings had settled into their new card, Lucy's body unfroze and the crowd around the table started shouting.

"Look at that! His Lordship's won by a whisker, his king beats the girl's jack," Mrs Milligan boomed.

"Oh, Lucy!" said Mrs Goodly, and burst into tears.

"He stole it! He stole my card!" yelled Lucy, leaping furiously to her feet. She flung the jack of hearts at Lord Grave and snatched up the king of hearts. "*This* was my card."

"Lucy," said Mr Goodly quietly. "It won't do any good. He won."

"But you must have seen what he did!"

Lord Grave stared at Lucy, his bushy eyebrows raised.

"What do you mean?" Mr Goodly said.

"The girl's a sore loser," someone in the crowd muttered. "What did she expect? Her winning streak was never going to last forever."

Lord Grave stood up. "Mrs Milligan, may we have some privacy, please? Move these dratted people away!" he bellowed.

"Of course, sir. Come now, everyone, get back to your own business."

The crowd shuffled and muttered back to the other card tables and the roulette wheel.

"Please – sit," said Lord Grave to Lucy.

"I'm fine standing, thanks."

Lord Grave shrugged and sat down. He lit another cigar. "Suit yourself," he said. "But we had a bet, fair and square. I demand my winnings."

Lucy wanted to yell that it was not fair and square at all. But it was clear that no one else had seen what happened. Should she say something? But who would believe her?

"You're going to hold us to it?" said Mr Goodly.

"You shouldn't have agreed to the bet if you weren't willing to take the risk."

"I won't go!" Lucy said.

Mr and Mrs Goodly stood either side of Lucy, each with an arm round her. "Of course not, dear girl," said Mr Goodly. "I'm sure his Lordship will see reason."

But Lord Grave didn't want to see reason. He didn't want to so much as touch it with the tip of his cigar. "I'm not going to allow you to wriggle out of it."

"You can't make us give Lucy up," said Mr Goodly.

"Perhaps we should call the parish constable to sort out the matter."

"We've done nothing wrong!" cried Mrs Goodly.

Lucy sat down. Her legs were trembling too much to hold her up. It was true. Her parents had done nothing wrong. But they were just ordinary people struggling to make their way in the world, while Lord Grave was rich and powerful. His sort always got what they wanted. And if he did call the parish constable, there might be an investigation into how a girl her age was managing to win so many poker games. And what if somehow they found out about the card? All three of them could end up in prison for fraud. They might even lose Leafy Ridge. Or perhaps everyone would think Lucy was a witch. They used to burn witches once. What if they still did?

Lucy sighed despairingly. She had no choice.

"Stop arguing. I'll go with him," she said in a quiet voice.

A hush fell over Mrs Milligan's Gambling Den. Lucy's parents stared at her, their eyes wide and frightened.

"He's right. He won the bet, fair and square," she said firmly, even though her insides were quaking.

"Wise decision! Mrs Milligan, my things, if you please!" boomed Lord Grave.

"Course, my Lord." Mrs Milligan shambled off, returning with a purple cloak and a silver walking stick.

Stupid show-off, thought Lucy. *"Why didn't he have a black cloak like a normal gentleman?*

"Come along, girl, don't shilly-shally. Mr and Mrs Goodly, I suppose you must be allowed to come and say goodbye."

The three Goodlys followed Lord Grave out of Mrs Milligan's Gambling Den and on to the street. Mr Goodly had a bad limp and used a walking stick.

Unlike Lord Grave's, his was made of plain wood and wasn't just for show. He moved clumsily, stumbling down the worn steps. Lucy put out a hand to help him, but found her own feet were none too steady.

At the bottom of the steps, Mrs Goodly sobbed as she hugged Lucy. Mr Goodly put his arms round both of them.

"You mustn't worry, my loves," he said. "I'll sort this out. We'll be back together soon, I promise."

Lucy wanted to believe him, but her father wasn't known for sorting things out. Nor her mother, for that matter. The only reason they hadn't all ended up in the workhouse – or dead from starvation – was because it was Lucy who had sorted things out. With the help of her card, she'd transformed the Goodlys' fortunes. She'd sort this mess out too, somehow.

"Goodbye then," Lucy said. She smiled bravely at her parents before climbing into the silver-grey carriage. Lord Grave climbed in after her, and slammed the door shut. Lucy huddled herself up in the corner of the black leather seat, as far away from him as she could get.

Lord Grave banged the roof with the top of his walking stick. The wheels creaked and the carriage bounced a little as it began to move over the cobbles. Lucy twisted in her seat so that she could wave a last goodbye to her parents through the narrow slit in the rear of the carriage. Although they were hopeless, she would miss them terribly. But Mr and Mrs Goodly didn't return Lucy's waves; they were already climbing up the steps back to Mrs Milligan's.

They're going to try and win enough money to get me back, Lucy decided. But how would they manage that? Without her around to take care of them, would they just land themselves into trouble trying to find a way to bring her home? The thought brought tears to her eyes.

Once her parents were out of sight and she had quietly dried her eyes, Lucy turned back round and stared out of the side window. After a while, she sneaked a glance at Lord Grave. He was doing some staring out of the window too, his head turned away from Lucy. Taking advantage of his distraction, Lucy subtly tried the door handle.

"It's locked," Lord Grave said, without even looking at her.

It was no use. She was trapped. Except perhaps for the time a few years ago when she'd had to use six slugs as a pillow because all the bedding was at the pawnshop, Lucy had never felt so miserable.

They soon left the grimy streets of London behind. Houses and buildings grew fewer and further apart until the horses were thundering along through the pitch-dark of the countryside with only the carriage lanterns to light their way.

As the coach rattled onwards, Lucy tried to work out what had really happened back in Mrs Milligan's Gambling Den. She patted her jacket pocket, checking that the card was safely there. Did Lord Grave have a card like hers too? If so, where did he get it from and did he know she had one too? Did he realise that she had seen what he'd done to win the poker game?

Lucy leaned back and closed her eyes, worn out

with misery and thinking. She must have fallen asleep for a little while, because when she next opened her eyes the sky was turning from black to a deep blue.

At last, the carriage slowed down before clattering to a halt. Huge iron gates, set into a hedge of fir trees dozens of feet high, loomed ahead through the thin, early morning mist. The horses snorted and shook their heads.

The two footmen riding on the back of the carriage jumped down. Or rather *clanked* down. They were wearing suits of armour. *Another of Lord Grave's stupid show-off ways*, Lucy thought, as she watched them lumber over to the horses and put black cloth bags over the animals' heads. She wanted to ask Lord Grave what they were doing, but she was determined to stick to her resolve and not speak to him. Ever. So she sat quietly while the armoured footmen finished hooding the horses, opened the gates and clanked through, leading the horses by their reins.

"It's going to be a glorious day once this mist clears," Lord Grave said, opening the coach window on his side.

Lucy folded her arms and looked straight ahead.

"Now listen, my girl," Lord Grave said. "I know you don't want to be here, but—"

The coach door on Lord Grave's side rattled. Two huge black paws hooked themselves over the top of the window and to Lucy's horror an enormous black animal lunged through it, grabbing the silver chain that fastened the neck of Lord Grave's cloak in its teeth. The coach door flew open. Lord Grave crashed to the ground. Then the beast growled, pounced and grabbed his Lordship's head between its massive jaws.

CHAPTER THREE

BATHSHEBA

Lucy scrambled out of the coach doorway that Lord Grave had been dragged from, skinning her knees and palms on the drive's sharp gravel.

Lord Grave made a choking noise.

The two armoured coachmen were still standing holding the horses' reins. They had their visors down. Couldn't they see what was happening?

"Do something!" she yelled at them.

His Lordship's face was still trapped between the beast's jaws. The growls took on a squelching quality. Lord Grave stopped making the choking noises, but his legs waggled up and down in mid-air, like a fly in its death throes.

A shaft of early morning sunlight pierced the mist and glittered on something red against the animal's neck. Not Lord Grave's blood, but a jewelled collar. Lucy hurled herself towards the collar and grabbed it. The jewels dug into the palms of her already sore hands, but she ignored the pain and tugged as hard as she could.

"Help me!" she screamed again at the two footmen. She wrenched at the collar desperately. With a wet *plop,* Lord Grave's head slid from the beast's jaws. But then the beast turned its gaze towards Lucy. Wide yellow eyes stared into hers. The half-open mouth revealed long white fangs dripping with frothy drool. In one smooth move, the creature curved round to face Lucy and thumped its paws against her shoulders, pinning her to the ground. It opened its mouth even wider, breath hot

against Lucy's cheek, dipped its head . . .

"No!" Lucy said in a voice that was smaller and squeakier than normal. "Please . . ."

The beast began licking Lucy's cheek, its tongue a thousand times scratchier than her father's beard when he kissed her goodnight.

"Bathsheba!" Lord Grave bellowed. "Get off her. Now!"

Bathsheba sprang away from Lucy. Lord Grave was on his feet again, brushing gravel and dust from his cloak. His eyebrows were pointing in different directions. Bathsheba leaped once more, locking her paws round Lord Grave's neck, who staggered backwards, but didn't fall this time.

"Help the girl up," Lord Grave ordered, in a strangled voice.

One of the footmen clanked over to Lucy and helped her to her feet, while Lord Grave took a piece of dried meat from somewhere underneath his cloak and threw it for Bathsheba to pounce on. She snarled, held the leathery strip of meat down with one paw and tore at it with her fangs.

That could have been my face, thought Lucy.

She began to tremble all over. She was so shaken up, she allowed Lord Grave to help her back into the coach.

"Thank you," she said, flopping down into her seat.

Lord Grave took out a silk handkerchief and handed it to her so she could mop the last of Bathsheba's drool from her face and clothes. "I suppose I should thank you too. That was foolhardy, but very brave. You weren't to know Bathsheba wouldn't harm me. It's just her way of welcoming me home," he said.

Lucy struggled with herself for a moment, but curiosity overcame her and she couldn't help asking, "What is it – she – Bathsheba?"

"A panther. From Kenya. We rescued her as a cub. Her mother was shot by hunters. I have many such animals here. Look, the giraffes are over there, looking for their breakfast."

Lucy peered through the mist. She could faintly see impossibly tall, long-necked, spindly-legged shadows moving gracefully past. There were noises too, splashing and snorting, coming from further away.

"What's that?"

"The elephants down by the lake. They like an early morning bath," Lord Grave said.

"Elephants *and* giraffes!" Lucy said. For a moment, excitement took the place of fear and anger. She'd never dreamed she might one day see such exotic animals in real life.

The coach set off again with Bathsheba ambling alongside. Lucy realised why the horses wore hoods. It was to stop them being spooked by the other animals as the coachmen led them through the wildlife park. After a while, the coach reached a gatehouse and on the other side of this, Lucy glimpsed Grave Hall for the first time. Mist still hung in the air, but she could make out a huge house with dozens of tall, slender chimneys and countless windows.

"Well, here we are," Lord Grave said. "Now. A word of warning. It's lucky you didn't try to run off while Bathsheba was welcoming me home. Things could have turned quite nasty. Bathsheba and some of my other animals have the potential to be very vicious. But as long as you abide by my rules, they won't harm you. I advise you to remember that."

Lucy nodded in what she hoped was an obedient way. But of course, she had no intention of abiding by any of Lord Grave's bossy rules. Not a single one. She was going to escape the first chance she got.

Vicious beasts or no vicious beasts.

The kitchen at Grave Hall was a long, low room. There was an enormous wooden table in the middle of the flagstone floor. A cooking range crouched in the fireplace. Pots and pans and bundles of herbs and strings of onions dangled from the ceiling.

"This is our cook, Mrs Bernie Crawley," Lord Grave said. He waved his hand towards the tall, broad-shouldered woman who stood with her back to them. She was stirring a small pot of what smelled like porridge simmering on the range.

The woman turned and smiled. "Welcome to Grave Hall, Lucy. We're all so glad you've come. It's always so exciting to find a—"

"New boot girl," said Lord Grave.

"Boot girl. Yes. Now, you must be hungry." Mrs Crawley wiped her hands on her apron.

"I'll take my breakfast later, Mrs Crawley. Until then I'm not to be disturbed," said Lord Grave.

"Shall I bring Lucy to you after she's eaten? I'm sure you'll wish to begin—"

"I'm not to be disturbed, Mrs Crawley." And with that, Lord Grave left the kitchen, Bathsheba padding after him.

Lucy realised she was staring at Mrs Crawley in a very rude way. She blinked and tried to find something else to focus on. The grey stone floor fitted the bill nicely.

"Something the matter?" Mrs Crawley asked, smoothing the full and glossy red beard that covered the bottom half of her face.

Lucy muttered at the floor. "You're a . . ."

"Of course I am!" Mrs Crawley brandished the wooden spoon she was holding. Blobs of porridge fell at Lucy's feet. "Lord Grave's a traditional man in many ways. The cook must always be known as 'Mrs', married or no, she or—"

"He?" said Lucy, finally looking up.

"Correct!"

Lucy wondered if it would also be rude to mention the fact that Mrs Crawley happened to be wearing a dress and a frilly white apron.

"Ah, you're puzzled by the frock. I prefer them, you see. Better airflow. It gets hot around the nether regions in this kitchen. And look at yourself, with your nice breeches. Very smart. We should wear what makes us feel comfortable. Agreed?"

"Agreed." Lucy smiled for the first time in hours. She had never liked dresses herself, preferring the practicality of breeches. But she could see why Mrs Crawley might feel the opposite way. And it was refreshing to meet someone else whose clothing choices were somewhat unusual.

"Sit yourself down here. It's almost six and time for the servants' breakfast."

Lucy settled herself at the long table. It had benches at each side and a chair at either end. Mrs

Crawley put a heavy silver teapot on the table and Lucy helped herself to a cup with milk and three sugars. She gulped it down, almost burning her tongue, and then poured another. While she was drinking it, the first of the servants arrived – a fair-haired girl, a year or two older than Lucy, carrying a ginger cat with a blue ribbon tied round its neck. The ends of the ribbon were damp and chewed-looking.

"Who are you?" the girl asked, peering sleepily at Lucy.

"Lucy, this is Becky Bone. Becky, this is Lucy Goodly. She's our new boot girl. You be good to her now. She'll be sharing your room."

Becky stuck out her bottom lip. "Why does she have to share with me?"

"Becky, don't you be so rude. You know all the other attic rooms are full of animal feed."

"Your cat's very sweet-looking," Lucy said, in an effort to be friendly. She wasn't entirely being truthful. The cat was scrawny. Its single eye was round, bulgy and bright orange. It had one and a half ears and the tip of its tail was missing. "What's its name?"

"He's called Smell," said Mrs Crawley.

Lucy laughed. "What a funny name. I've got a cat at home called Phoebe. But she's a bit younger than your Smell I think?"

"He's not called Smell!" snapped Becky. "He's called Aloysius."

"But Smell's so much more fitting," chortled Mrs Crawley.

Smell wriggled out of Becky's arms and trotted over to Lucy. As he stood there, blinking up at her with his single orange eye, he made a very small tooting noise, like the world's tiniest trumpet.

"Oh," said Lucy, wrinkling her nose. Now she understood why Smell was called Smell.

"It means he likes you!" said Mrs Crawley brightly. Becky scowled even harder at Lucy.

Another girl came into the kitchen, singing quietly to herself.

"This is Violet, she's our scullery maid. She comes in from Grave Village to help me with the cooking," said Mrs Crawley. "Violet, this is Lucy, the new boot girl."

Violet smiled shyly at Lucy as she sat down. She was much younger than Becky, perhaps eight or nine. Wisps of mousy brown hair escaped from her white cotton cap. She began fiddling with her spoon, still singing softly.

"Oh, shut that noise up, Violet," Becky said, when Mrs Crawley's back was turned. "This one's a right milksop. She's scared of everything, you know. Cries if you look at her wrong."

Lucy didn't reply, but suspected Becky probably did a lot worse to Violet than "look at her wrong".

A very short, curly-haired man was the last servant to arrive for breakfast. He wore a white shirt and a black waistcoat and trousers.

"Ah, you're the new boot girl. I'm Jacob Vonk, the butler."

Violet piped up, "And the gardener. And the beekeeper and—"

"That's right, thank you, Violet. It's true, I wear lots of different hats, as they say."

"He's got a whole cupboard of them!" Violet added.

"Everyone calls me Vonk," said Vonk. He smiled broadly and shook Lucy's hand warmly before settling himself into the chair at the head of the table. His feet in their very shiny shoes didn't quite reach the floor and Lucy guessed he was smaller than she was.

"Some of your porridge would do very well now, Mrs C."

"Pleasure, Vonk." Mrs Crawley ladled porridge into bowls. It looked pale and creamy, but there were funny black specks in it. Lucy fished one of them out with her spoon, trying to work out if it was burnt porridge.

"Mrs Crawley," said Vonk in a stern voice.

"What is it?" said Mrs Crawley in a light, airy *what-on-earth-are-you-talking-about?* voice.

"The garnish. You know what we agreed. No experimental porridge."

"It's extra nourishment, Vonk. There's lots of hungry people in the world and not enough food to go round. Now insects, they—"

Vonk raised an eyebrow.

"Oh, very well!" Mrs Crawley snatched the bowls of porridge away and replaced them with insect-free portions. She heaped her own porridge with the tiny black corpses. "I toasted them especially for Lucy," she said, crunching sadly on a mouthful.

"Well I could try one, maybe," said Lucy, feeling rather sorry for Mrs Crawley.

"Oh, marvellous." Mrs Crawley sprinkled a couple of the black specks into Lucy's palm.

Lucy closed her eyes and licked the insects up, swallowing them quickly. "They taste a bit . . . er . . . lemony," she said, coughing.

"Yes, that's exactly it. They're ants, you know. More?"

"Um. No, I think I've had enough. They're very filling."

Once everyone had finished eating, Mrs Crawley began telling Becky and Violet their tasks for the day. Lucy only half listened as she was thinking about her parents again. They'd probably be getting ready for bed now at the Charm Inn where they always stayed when in town. Would they remember to put their money and valuables under their pillows and lock the door while they slept? The Charm Inn was full of terrible thieves who would steal the breath from your lungs, but her parents always insisted on staying there. In fact, half the terrible thieves were her parents' best friends. They really were hopeless!

Small, warm fingers touched Lucy's wrist.

"Don't fret, Lucy. Everyone here's really nice and we don't have to work too hard," Violet said, looking up at her. "If you're feeling lonely, you could borrow Caruthers. He always makes me feel better." Violet took something out of her apron pocket. It was a small green knitted frog with button eyes. Violet's name was neatly embroidered on its underneath.

Lucy smiled. "He's lovely. Did you do the embroidery?"

"No, that was my mum. She's very clever with a needle. She works as a seamstress."

"Well, thanks for the offer, but I think I'll manage all right at the moment, so you keep hold of Caruthers for now."

"Silly pair of milksops," said Becky Bone, giving

them both a disgusted look.

When Becky and Violet had gone off to begin work, Vonk showed Lucy to her new room, high up in the attics of Grave Hall.

"This is your bed," he pointed to a small metal bedstead, one of two in the room. "Rest today. You can start work properly tomorrow. Lord Grave told me you've been up for most of the night."

When Vonk had left, Lucy explored the little room. From the window, she could see the full extent of the wildlife park now the mist had cleared. As well as the elephants and giraffes, she spotted many other animals she'd never seen before, not even in books.

It didn't take long for Lucy to familiarise herself with the rest of her new bedroom. Apart from the two beds, two bedside tables and a chest of drawers, there was nothing else other than a black iron fireplace. The tiles surrounding the inside of the fireplace had a different design on each side. One side showed a man sitting with a book on his knees, the other a man smoking a long, curved pipe.

Lucy took the trick playing card from her jacket

and put it in the drawer of her bedside table before pulling her boots off and lying down. Although she'd been up all night, she was certain she didn't feel sleepy. There was too much to think about. She'd just close her eyes for five minutes before planning how to escape Grave Hall.

Two minutes later, she was fast asleep.

So she didn't notice when the tile man with the pipe climbed out of his side of the fireplace and joined the tile man with the book on the other side.

"Well, Mr Paige," said the man with the pipe to the man with the book, "do you think his Lordship might be right about her?"

CHAPTER FOUR

PORTRAIT OF A LADY

"Come on, Goodly, time to get up," said a voice in Lucy's ear shortly after dawn the next morning.

"Urgh," Lucy said and turned over. She'd slept until lunchtime the previous day and then hadn't been able to sleep that night. And she wasn't used to such an early start. Gambling for a living often meant going to bed in the mornings and getting up in the evenings, an arrangement Lucy was quite happy with.

"Come on!" This time a sharp pinch on Lucy's cheek accompanied the impatient voice.

"Get off!" Lucy said, swatting the pinching fingers away. She opened her eyes. Becky Bone was staring down at her.

"If you miss breakfast, don't blame me," Becky said, poking her tongue out at Lucy before leaving the bedroom.

After stumbling into the kitchen for a bowl of Mrs Crawley's porridge (and declining the offer of another portion of toasted ants), Lucy made her way to the boot room to start her new job.

She sighed as she began scraping the mud off the boots and shoes Lord Grave had left out the previous night. It was a horrible messy task and as she scraped and scraped she got angrier and angrier.

Why should she have to clean Lord Grave's stupid boots? She might be stuck at Grave Hall until she found a way of escaping, but that didn't mean she had to obey him or slave away for him. She owed him nothing. He'd cheated. Even more than her. And anyway, she'd cheated so she could feed her family. He had no such excuse.

In the end, she flung the boots into a corner, sat down on the floor and folded her arms. There she stayed until Becky Bone came in to check on her.

"His Lordship will be fuming," Becky said, eyeing the pile of still dirty footwear.

"Clean them yourself if you're bothered," Lucy said.

"Oh, hoity-toity toffee-nose," said Becky, pushing the tip of her own nose up with her finger.

"That makes you look like a pig. Suits you," Lucy said. She stormed out of the boot room and into the hallway. Mrs Crawley had shown her around part of Grave Hall the previous day. Lucy remembered her saying the drawing room was where Lord Grave spent much of his time so she strode over to the drawing-room door and barged inside without bothering to knock.

Everything went instantly dark, as though the world had suddenly ended.

Lucy panicked for a few seconds until she realised a duster had fallen on her head and was hanging over her eyes. She'd opened the door to a cupboard full of brooms and buckets and other cleaning implements.

"Are you lost?" said a voice behind her. Lucy plucked the duster off her head and turned. It was Lord Grave. Bathsheba was at his heels.

"No. But I want to talk to you." She slammed the broom cupboard shut.

"It's not usual for a servant to make demands of her master," Lord Grave snapped. "But follow me."

Lucy followed Lord Grave and Bathsheba into the drawing room. He closed the door behind them. Then he sat down in one of the leather armchairs next to the fireplace. Bathsheba's yellow eyes blinked sleepily at Lucy, but there was a dangerous glint in them. The panther yawned widely, as though she was taking the opportunity to demonstrate the sharpness of her fangs.

"Well?" Lord Grave said.

"I'm not going to work for you. I won't clean your dirty boots or anything else. You can't make me."

Lord Grave opened a silver box, which sat on the side table next to his chair. He took out a cigar and a round piece of metal with a hole in the middle. He put the end of the cigar through the hole and pressed the side of the instrument. A blade sliced the end of the cigar off.

"I could make things very difficult for you. You've cheated at cards many times. I wonder what your victims would say if they found out?"

Lucy clasped her hands together behind her back to stop them shaking. Did this mean he knew about her card? "I haven't a clue what you're talking about," she said aloud.

"You're not fooling me, Lucy. You'll stay here and do as you're told. Do you want to see your parents end up in prison, let alone yourself?"

"We haven't done anything wrong. Why do you want me to stay here?"

Lord Grave got out of his chair and put his cigar in the black leather cigar case he carried in his pocket. "I don't have to explain myself to you. Now get back to work."

Lord Grave and Bathsheba strode out of the drawing room, passing Becky, who bustled in armed with brooms and cloths and bottles of polish.

"Hope he told you what's what, Goodly. We need to get on with cleaning this room." She thrust a cloth at Lucy. "You dust the mantelpiece while I sweep the hearth."

Lucy swallowed down her hatred of Lord Grave, snatched the cloth from Becky and began dusting. Outside, the sky darkened and rain rattled against the windows, as though the weather had decided to match Lucy's bad mood.

A large painting hung above the mantelpiece. It showed a young woman. Her elaborately curled dark hair had an unusual white streak in the front. Her long dress was pale blue. The baby she held on her lap was chewing on a silver teething ring, which had a charm dangling from it. Lucy peered closely at the portrait and saw that the charm was a swan.

"Who are they?" Lucy asked.

Becky scowled and continued sweeping. "Lady Grave and little Lord Grave."

"His Lordship's wife and son?"

"Of course. Nitwit."

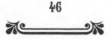

Lucy gritted her teeth. "But where are they now?"

"Too many questions, Goodly."

"Are they—?"

"Dead?" said another voice. Vonk stood in the doorway. "Yes. Lady Grave died from a fever not long after the portrait was painted. The young Lord Grave departed five years ago when he was only seven. A great tragedy for his Lordship. He's never really recovered from it." Vonk strode across the red carpet, stopping in front of the portrait.

Becky, who had instantly leaped back to her dustpan and brush when Vonk appeared, smirked. "I told her to stop asking questions."

"Sorry, Vonk," said Lucy. Perhaps the two tragedies partly explained why Lord Grave was so horrible, although that still didn't excuse him.

Vonk raised his eyebrows. "Not a crime to be curious. Sign of intelligence."

Becky dropped her brush with a clatter on to the marble hearth and muttered under her breath.

"It's a beautiful painting, don't you think?" Vonk said.

"Yes," Lucy agreed. Then she noticed that something unusual was happening to the portrait. Orange-red flames were flickering in Lady Grave's eyes. This startled Lucy for a moment, until she realised Becky had lit the lamps that hung on the opposite wall. The reflection of the flames reminded Lucy of the night she'd stolen the card. She shivered and crossed her arms over her chest as she remembered. It had happened over two years ago, just before her tenth birthday . . .

She was standing sleepily at the back of a rundown gambling den, waiting for her parents to lose yet another card game. The doors of the gambling den creaked open and a blast of cold air whipped in from outside. Lucy stared as the woman who had entered the den made her way to the poker tables. She wore a fine, warm-looking scarlet coat with black velvet frogging down the front and a red hat with a red veil. Her hair was red too and fell loosely around her shoulders. The woman smiled at Lucy as she passed.

Lucy's sleepiness vanished. *It's her again.* She'd

seen the woman, whom she'd nicknamed Lady Red, several times over the past few weeks in various gambling dens.

"Good evening, everyone," said Lady Red. She sailed past the table Lucy's parents were sitting at and settled herself at a table further down the room where a game had just finished. The other poker players gaped at the well-dressed new arrival. Most of them were as rundown as the gambling den.

A new round of poker began. As the cards were dealt, Lucy quietly made her way across the room until she stood just behind Lady Red's chair.

Lady Red lost the first game. But then something strange happened. The same something strange Lucy saw last time she watched this mysterious woman play poker. The cards in Lady Red's hand went blank. A few seconds later, they became new cards. Cards that won the poker game instantly. Last time Lucy had witnessed this amazing trick, she had noticed something else. The edge of a playing card poking out from Lady Red's sleeve.

The other players, who had noticed nothing amiss,

muttered angrily as they discovered they had lost the game.

"Another round?" one particularly grubby individual asked.

Lady Red declined, as Lucy expected she would. She only ever stayed for one or two hands of poker.

"How does she do it?" Lucy muttered to herself as Lady Red gathered up the notes and coins she'd won, and pushed back her chair, which banged straight into Lucy.

"Oh, I'm sorry, sweet child, I didn't see you there! Are you hurt?"

"No, I'm fine," Lucy said, hoping the woman wouldn't guess she'd been spying.

"Well, that's a relief. In that case, I wonder if you'd mind helping me to my coach?" Lady Red said as she finished stuffing her winnings into a fancy silk bag. "I'm wearing most unsuitable shoes for this icy weather." She lifted her long skirts to show a pair of dainty scarlet velvet shoes with a high pointed heel. "I'll reward you, of course."

Lucy agreed instantly. They made their way

outside, where Lucy took the woman's arm and helped her to the black carriage that was waiting. It was drawn by a fine dark horse, its breath steaming in the cold air. The driver was so bundled up against the cold that all that Lucy could see of him was the tip of his nose.

Lady Red stopped at the bottom of the carriage steps. "I have an idea. Why don't you hop in with me? We could go to my house. Have cocoa and toast in front of the fire. I'll still give you a coin too, of course."

Lucy's empty stomach rumbled at the thought of cocoa and toast. She and her parents hadn't eaten a proper meal in days. But Lady Red had something Lucy wanted even more than food. The thought of what she was about to do made her tremble. It wasn't in her nature to thieve, but Lucy was truly desperate.

"That would be lovely, thank you," Lucy said. But she didn't move.

"Wonderful. Hurry up now, it's cold. You get in first."

"I've never ridden in a carriage before. Do I just

go up these steps?" Lucy asked, trying to sound bewildered.

"Why don't I help you in?" Lady Red spoke very slowly, as though Lucy was three years old. "Take my hand."

Lucy took the woman's gloved hand in her own rough cold one. And just as she had hoped, Lucy saw a playing card poking out from the bottom of Lady Red's sleeve. Lucy snatched it and pulled herself free. For a split second, Lucy's eyes met Lady Red's, which blazed suddenly like tiny twin suns.

Lucy turned and ran.

And ran.

And ran some more.

Lady Red tried to run after her. But she hadn't been lying about her shoes being useless in the snow. She slipped and fell.

"Treeves, after her!" Lady Red yelled. This was followed by the creak of wheels and the crunch of ice as the carriage began to move. But Lucy knew the alleyways and backstreets to dart down, all of them so narrow the vehicle would never squeeze through, so it didn't take her long to shake off her pursuer.

*

Lucy told no one about the card, not even her parents. It took her a lot of practice to work out how to use it. And even when she did, it was a long time before she plucked up the courage to gamble with it. But when she eventually did, her nightmare life of poverty, hunger and cold soon ended. Her parents quickly began to let her take charge of things, never questioning her about her newfound skill. Although Lucy earned enough to make the Goodlys' lives comfortable and carefree, she wasn't greedy or reckless. She made sure she lost a few games to avoid suspicion. And she never played opponents who were as poor as she once was.

Lucy was also careful never to visit dens where she'd seen Lady Red. She always feared the woman would find her somehow. But she never did, except in Lucy's dreams, when she would open the door of Lucy's bedroom, eyes burning in that unnatural way.

"Give it back. Give it back!" she'd shout.

For a while, Lucy couldn't sleep for fear of

Lady Red making an appearance. But as she was a sensible girl who always tried to find a solution to her problems, she soon trained herself to get out of bed in her dreams and slam the door in Lady Red's face. Eventually the nightmares went away.

"Something wrong?" said Vonk.

Lucy blinked herself back into the present. "No. You're right, it *is* a lovely painting. Lady Grave's got a very kind face."

"Yes. Lady Tabitha was one of the best. She loved animals, couldn't bear to see them mistreated. She persuaded his Lordship to bring Bathsheba home. She rescued the elephants from a circus. And so on. Now, back to your work, girls." Vonk turned and strode out of the room, the ring of his shoes on the tiled hallway gradually fading into the distance.

"You've gone a funny colour," said Becky.

"Have I?"

"Urgh, have you got some revolting disease? Maybe it's that nose-rotting one. I read all about it. Your nose goes mouldy and then drops off. Be an improvement in your case."

CHAPTER FIVE

HIDING BEHIND A RHINOCEROS

earing a full suit of armour in the middle of summer really was no fun, but it was better than being eaten alive by a panther or squashed to death by an elephant. Lucy tried to comfort herself with this thought as she opened the gate set into the spiked iron fence that separated Grave Hall from his Lordship's wildlife park. She was pushing a wheelbarrow of straw.

Lucy's second day at Grave Hall was turning out to

be even worse than her first. Lord Grave had ordered that one of her new duties was to feed Bathsheba and clean out the wooden hut the giant cat slept in at night.

Lucy closed the gate behind her. Bathsheba, who'd been snoozing in the afternoon sun, leaped to her paws when she spotted the bucket of raw meat that was hooked over one handle of the wheelbarrow.

"Keep back!" Lucy said. She slung the bucket's contents on to the ground. Bathsheba pounced on it, growling her appreciation. For such an elegant animal, the panther had deplorable table manners. She chomped her meat so loudly she scared off some of Lord Grave's parrots who were roosting in a nearby tree.

Lucy reluctantly set about cleaning the hut, which was almost as big as Leafy Ridge. She picked up gnawed bones from Bathsheba's previous meals and changed the dirty straw for the fresh. The armour made her movements stiff and awkward. The white feather plume on the top of Lucy's helmet bobbed up and down annoyingly and she grew hotter and hotter inside her metal second skin.

When she'd finally finished her work, and Bathsheba had torn and swallowed the last of the meat, Lucy returned to the Grave Hall side of the fence. She took off her helmet, put it on top of the smelly contents of her wheelbarrow and began toiling back to the house.

If she hadn't been slowly cooking inside her armour, it might have been pleasant wandering along in the warm sun with the elephants trumpeting to each other in the distance. Homesickness washed over Lucy. On days like this at home, she and her parents would sit outside after supper and watch Phoebe chasing dragonflies.

Why did Lord Grave want to keep her here against her will? Was it just because it meant he had a boot girl he didn't need to pay? Or could there be some other more sinister reason? It was all very worrying. The urge to run away was so strong it made her stomach hurt. She'd spent most of last night trying to think of a getaway plan. But Lucy's usual resourcefulness seemed to have taken a holiday.

Every solution she came up with had a fatal flaw, such as wild animals mauling her or the police dragging her off to prison for cheating at cards.

I'm trapped here.

The thought made her feel panicky and very alone. If only her parents were more reliable. Shouldn't they be coming up with a plan to rescue her? But then again, even if they came up with one, it probably wouldn't work.

A rumbling noise interrupted Lucy's musings. She looked up. The sky was an innocent blue, with not a single cloud in sight.

The rumbling rumbled more loudly.

It seemed to be coming from the front of the house. Lucy abandoned her wheelbarrow and clattered round to the main entrance to see what was going on. When she got there, everything looked as it usually did – the stone pillars at either side of the huge front door with its gleaming lion's head knocker looked solid and upright. The gravel drive was neat and weed-free.The bushes that lined it were expertly trimmed into the shape of Lord

Grave's favourite animals, all thanks to Vonk.

The rumbling rumbled some more.

Then a slash appeared a few feet above the drive. It was as though someone had painted a bright ragged line in mid-air.

Lucy flung herself behind a rhinoceros-shaped topiary. Of course, she soon discovered that flinging oneself while wearing armour is a not very sensible course of action. She ended up lying in a tangled metal heap behind the rhino. Once she'd struggled into a crouching position, Lucy could see that the slash hanging above the drive had widened. Now it was more of a hole than a slash. Lucy could feel the rumbling coming from it. Her armour rattled.

Then, as the rumbling reached a crescendo, four horses pulling a black carriage galloped out of the hole. Their manes and tails were soft and fluffy, more like thistledown than horsehair. And there was something odd growing out of their shoulders. Lucy gawped as she realised they were wings – elegant, transparent wings, which reflected tiny beads of colour where the sunlight touched them.

Lucy cowered further behind the rhinoceros, her metal-gloved hand over her mouth.

Water began trickling through the hole, spattering the gravel. The trickle became a gush, and the gush became a wave carrying a small sailing boat. The wave broke, landing the boat on the gravel. Seawater foamed over the drive and trickled towards Lucy before drying up as quickly as it had appeared. A gangplank shot out from the side of the boat and a man and a woman disembarked. Both had silvery hair and were dressed in navy blue. The silver-haired people strode over to the carriage and began speaking to whoever or whatever was inside.

Lucy began unfastening her armour as quietly as she could. Her fingers trembled and by the time she'd undone all the buckles, the strange people gathering on the drive had made their way inside the hall. Lucy sprinted out from behind the rhinoceros, round to the back of the house and into the kitchen. Becky Bone was there, sitting in Vonk's chair at the head of the kitchen table and poring over the latest edition of the *Penny Dreadful*. Becky loved the *Penny*

Dreadful, which was full of what Vonk described as a steaming pile of utter nonsense. Smell was curled up on Becky's lap.

"Where's Mrs Crawley?" asked Lucy, gasping for breath.

Becky didn't look up from the *Penny*. "Gone down to the village on her penny-farthing. She's getting her beard trimmed. That little sap Violet has gone with her."

"I just saw the strangest thing. These people just arrived and—"

"What people?"

"They've gone inside now, but . . . well, come and see."

"This better not be some stupid trick, Goodly. There's another child gone missing, you know. Eddie Robinson, he's called." Becky held up the paper. It had the headline:

ANOTHER MISSING CHILD!

Below the headline was a drawing of a boy with untidy hair and a mole on his left cheek.

"The *Penny* thinks they're all being eaten by

flesh-eating zombies," Becky said.

"Never mind that! Come on!"

Becky sighed loudly, but she put the *Penny Dreadful* down and gently moved Smell off her lap. He yawned and stretched before following the two girls out of the kitchen.

"What am I supposed to be looking at?" Becky said when the three of them reached the front of the house.

"Those horses! That boat!"

Becky folded her arms. "What are you talking about, boot girl? There's nothing there. I wish some zombie would eat you, you pea brain." She tutted and stomped off back to the kitchen and the *Penny*. Smell didn't immediately follow her. He gazed up at Lucy, considering her with his unblinking orange eye, before trotting slowly off.

Lucy stared at the carriage and the boat. One of the winged horses neighed. Why was she seeing things Becky couldn't? Perhaps her brain was fibbing to her due to lack of sleep and too much worry.

Lucy suddenly glimpsed movement in the corner

of her eye. She turned and shrieked. A monster stood next to her. It had a pointed head with round bulging metal eyes. Lucy watched, horrified, as the monster grabbed its own head and began to pull it off . . . Under that head was another head.

Lucy made a strangled noise of relief.

"Oh dear. Did my helmet scare you? I cobbled it together myself, you know. It's for checking the bees," Vonk said. "What are you doing here?"

"I came to . . ." She gestured towards the horses and the carriage and the boat.

Vonk frowned. "Yes?"

Vonk couldn't see them either!

"I . . . er . . . wanted some fresh air."

Vonk smiled at her as if she'd just done something really very good. "I see. Well, it's nearly suppertime. Mrs Crawley's left us some cold cuts. Although I fear they may be accompanied by an experimental salad. Let's go in."

CHAPTER SIX

EVERLASTING SOUP AND CHICKEN-WITH-MORE-BODY-PARTS-THAN-MIGHT-BE-REASONABLY-EXPECTED

That night, Lucy tossed and turned in her squeaky iron bedstead.

When she finally fell asleep, it was nearly time to get up again and she overslept. Because she was so late, she skipped breakfast and went straight to the boot room, albeit reluctantly. She counted twenty-six pairs of shoes and boots for polishing. They couldn't all be Lord Grave's, because they were all different sizes and some were women's shoes. Perhaps they belonged to the silver-haired woman she'd seen the night before. But if the woman was real, the rest of what she'd seen must be real too . . .

Lucy picked up a boot and began scraping the mud and dirt off it, all the time thinking about the bewildering events of the last two days.

Playing cards that came to life and changed places with each other.

A grumpy Lord, who threatened to have the Goodly family put in prison.

Flying carriages pulled by winged horses.

Boats sailing in mid-air.

Grave Hall was clearly a far from normal place. Although Lucy was partly intrigued by what she'd seen, she was also alarmed and wanted to escape back to her parents as soon as possible. "Get thinking, Goodly. Make a plan," she muttered.

Six pairs of shoes in, when the only thing Lucy was in danger of developing was a shoe-polish-induced headache, Violet the scullery maid opened the boot -room door.

"I'll help you if you like. Mrs Crawley said I could," she said shyly.

"Thanks, Violet," Lucy smiled.

Violet pulled up a stool and sat next to Lucy. Before she started work, the little girl took out Caruthers, whispered something to the woolly amphibian, then put him back in her apron pocket. Lucy bit back a smile. She didn't want to be like Becky and laugh at Violet, but she really was a most peculiar little girl. Though her sweetness and warmth meant Lucy couldn't help but like her.

For a time, the two girls cleaned in silence, the only noises coming from the rub of brush and cloth on leather.

"So these aren't all Lord Grave's shoes, are they?" Lucy eventually asked, in a casual sort of voice.

"Mrs Crawley told me some guests arrived yesterday. Lord Grave isn't very happy though. He doesn't like visitors."

"I bet he doesn't. He's not a very nice man, is he?"

Violet stopped cleaning the green scaly boot she was working on. "Mrs Crawley says that he's grumpy and sad because of Lady and little Lord Grave dying. She says he doesn't mean anything by it."

"Hmm. Violet, did you see the guests arrive last night?"

"I wasn't here, I'd gone down to the village with Mrs Crawley and then I went home. Why?"

"Oh, nothing really. Just curious."

Violet resumed her cleaning. "This leather is very odd. I think it smells a little bit of fish!"

Lucy and Violet were exhausted by the time they staggered into the kitchen, where Mrs Crawley was alone, eating an omelette. Smell was sitting on the table next to Mrs Crawley's plate, eyeing up the food and licking his lips hopefully.

"I'm trying a new recipe. Banana and anchovy omelette topped with flaked sprout. Would you girls like some? You must be hungry after all those boots. Or bread and milk? Smell, get away now, you know eggs don't agree with your digestion!"

"Bread and milk, please," Lucy said.

"Me too!" Violet added quickly.

Lucy fetched them both some milk from the pitcher in the larder and cut thick slices of crusty bread before sitting down.

"There were so many boots," Lucy kept her eyes on her food. "I think I saw one of the guests arrive yesterday, actually. In a very unusual carriage. The horses were . . . different from any I've ever seen."

"Oh, that'll be Lady Sybil. She breeds the horses herself. Swift as birds, they are." Mrs Crawley beamed at Lucy, displaying a sprout flake stuck between her front teeth. Except for the sprout flake, it was the same sort of smile Vonk had given her last night. A *well done you!* type of smile.

Lucy ate the rest of her lunch in silence, pondering what could possibly be going on. She was swallowing the last crumb when Becky came into the kitchen, scowling as usual.

"When you've finished filling your cakehole, there's work to be done. We need to brush the stair carpet."

"Oh no," said Mrs Crawley, snatching her empty

plate out of reach of Smell's tongue. "Change of plan. I need all hands on deck. His Lordship's holding a formal dinner party tonight for his guests."

"I'll be needing my best uniform, if I'm waiting at table," said Becky, straightening her cap and very nearly smiling.

"Lucy, you'll be waiting at table too." Mrs Crawley paused. "In fact, I think Becky can stay and help me and Violet in the kitchen. Lucy, you and Vonk can manage service between you."

Becky's face turned an interesting shade of purple. "Her? But she's only the boot girl! Boot girls don't—"

"Becky Bone!" Mrs Crawley drew herself up to her full six foot three and a quarter inches and looked quite menacing. "When you're housekeeper-cum-cook then you can say who does what and when. Until then, I decide."

Becky opened her mouth and then closed it again. But she gave Lucy a filthy glare.

Lord Grave's dining room was the grandest room in the house. It looked even grander lit by the dozens of candles that sat in holders on the wooden-panelled walls and sparkled from the crystal chandelier that dangled above the long dining table.

All the food for Lord Grave's guests was lined up on a sideboard that stood against the wall. It was Lucy's job to help Vonk serve it up. The first course was a very curious soup. Not only was it a rather odd purple colour (despite the fact Vonk had told Mrs Crawley she couldn't serve any experimental food this evening), but it appeared to be everlasting. Vonk was serving it from a silver tureen barely big enough to hold a single serving of soup. Lucy couldn't understand how it could hold enough for everyone.

But each time Vonk dipped his ladle in, it came out full. He ladled the liquid into soup plates, which Lucy then carried to the table, trying her best not to spill any down the necks of the diners.

Vonk had told her who each of the four guests were. There was a sorrowful-looking man called Lord Percy. Sitting next to him was Lady Sibyl, the owner of the black carriage. She was a tall woman made even taller by her hair, which was piled high on her head and topped off with two very large peacock feathers. Lucy kept feeling as though the eyes in the feathers were watching her.

The other two guests were the people Lucy had seen disembarking from the boat yesterday. The woman's name was Prudence Beguildy and the man's Beguildy Beguildy, which made Lucy giggle. Perhaps his parents had been too lazy to think of a proper first name. They were twins. Prudence Beguildy's hairstyle was very similar to Lady Sibyl's, but decorated with a small model ship in full sail. Beguildy Beguildy wore a smart naval uniform. The jacket had gold braid and buttons and what looked like upside-down gilt hairbrushes on the shoulders.

When it was time to serve the main course, Vonk whipped the lid off a silver platter. Crouching underneath was a small roast chicken not much bigger than Smell.

"But that'll never serve everyone," Lucy

whispered to Vonk. "Isn't Mrs Crawley going to send up some more?"

Vonk didn't reply. He just winked at Lucy and began sharpening his carving knife. And although the roast chicken seemed exactly as a roast chicken should, crispy-skinned and delicious-smelling with the usual number of body parts, Lucy lost count of the numbers of wings and legs and breasts she served up.

Once the guests had finished their main course, Vonk and Lucy began clearing the table in preparation for dessert. By then, Lord Grave and his guests seemed to have forgotten Lucy was there, and as she went to and fro from the dining room to the kitchen and back again, she caught snippets of their conversation, which grew increasingly tense.

"I know you've asked us not to speak of it, but I have to make my feelings plain. Ma'am needs you..." said Lord Percy as Lucy carried out the side plates.

"...you say that, Lord Grave, but what about your recent actions?" said Lady Sibyl as Lucy came back in to clear the dinner plates piled with bones from the chicken-with-more-body-parts-than-might-be-reasonably-expected. She had to be careful as Bathsheba, who had been asleep under the table, was now standing on her hind legs, trying to hook her claws round the leftovers.

". . . take her because of Ma'am," Lord Grave was saying rather huffily as Lucy returned with dessert plates. "I simply wish to ensure—" He stopped when he saw Lucy. She badly wanted to stay and hear more, but she had to go back to the kitchen as she'd forgotten the spoons. As she was coming back into the dining room with them, she heard Prudence Beguildy say, ". . . Ma'am must act now that we have Eddie Robinson . . ."

Lucy dropped all the dessert forks and spoons she was holding and they clattered to the floor. Prudence Beguildy instantly stopped speaking. Lord Grave glared at Lucy.

"Sorry, your Lordship," Lucy said as she bent to pick up the cutlery, glad of an excuse to hide her shock.

Eddie Robinson!

He was the boy in the *Penny Dreadful*, the latest child to be kidnapped.

Working as quickly as she could, Lucy distributed the silverware. The candles in the dining room were beginning to burn down now, making Lord Grave's face and the faces of his guests look shadowy and sinister. Even Prudence Beguildy's hairstyle looked eerie in the dim light. Lucy imagined she could see tiny faces looking out of the portholes of the boat, their faces set in a scream.

The guests' silence continued when Vonk swept in, holding a bowl of miraculously tall and wobbly sherry trifle. He looked rather puzzled as he set the trifle on the table, as though he'd expected the guests to applaud the magnificent dessert and was perplexed by the silence.

"We'll see to ourselves now," said Lord Grave. "You can clear away when we've retired to the drawing room."

"Of course," said Vonk. "Come along, Lucy."

Lucy desperately wanted to escape to her room to think about what she had just heard, so was

disappointed to find that whatever uncanny forces had created the everlasting soup and the chicken-with-more-body-parts-than-might-be-reasonably-expected, hadn't bothered to do the washing up. There were dishes and saucepans scattered everywhere. Smell was taking advantage of the confusion to lick all the plates clean.

Mrs Crawley clapped her hands, "Smell, get away. I can't cope with a week of after effects from you. Lucy, you can begin drying the dishes Becky's washed, please. I've sent Violet home; she was worn out."

Lucy sighed and grabbed a tea towel. Becky at once began criticising her drying up method. Lucy ignored her and wandered off inside her own head, trying to understand what it was she had seen and heard at the dinner party.

Lucy was sure that she was the child Lord Grave was talking about; the child he'd said he'd taken. But what did Prudence Beguildy mean by *now we have Eddie Robinson*?

Did it mean . . . could it mean . . . that Lord Grave

and his dinner-party guests had taken Eddie? And if they'd taken Eddie, what about the other missing children? Where were they now? Had they been handed over to the woman they all called 'Ma'am'? Had Lord Grave taken Lucy from her parents for the same reason? Was she too going to end up in the clutches of the mysterious and no doubt villainous Ma'am too?

Lucy finished drying the lid she was holding. When she put it back on the dish it belonged to, her shaking hand made it rattle.

"Are you all right, Lucy?" Mrs Crawley said.

"Fine, thanks. Just a bit worn out." But Lucy felt as far from fine as it was possible to be. What was she going to do?

CHAPTER SEVEN

TICKLING LORD GRAVE'S GREAT-GRANDMOTHER'S CHINS

E veryone was tired the next morning and very
grumpy. Lucy had spent the night fruitlessly
trying to think of an escape plan. Mrs Crawley
was so exhausted from last night's cooking,
she hadn't even bothered to take her beard out of the
three plaits she wore it in for bed. Violet was sitting
at the kitchen table, polishing the silver. Every now
and then she would lay her head on the table, using
Caruthers as a cushion.

Lucy and Becky were dispatched to clean the drawing room. Lucy followed Becky out of the kitchen and upstairs. Becky barrelled towards the drawing room, griping about Mrs Crawley as she went.

"Don't see why I should have to clean the drawing room again. I reckon those insects she's been scoffing have infested her brain. Probably eating it . . ."

Becky was so distracted, she didn't realise that Lucy wasn't right behind her, but was loitering in the hallway. There were voices coming from the landing above. Maybe she'd be able to overhear something useful that might explain what had happened to Eddie and what might happen to her if she didn't manage to escape before Lord Grave handed her to Ma'am. It was risky, but she had to do something!

Lucy ran up the stairs. When she reached the first-floor landing, she heard the voices again. A spindly-legged black cabinet painted with gold and silver dragons stood beside the stairs. Lucy squeezed herself behind it and watched as Lord Grave and the sorrowful-looking man made their way along the east wing corridor.

When she was sure they wouldn't spot her, Lucy left her hiding place and crept after their Lordships. The corridor split into two and the men veered left. When they were out of sight, Lucy ran in the same direction, the thick carpet muffling her steps. She followed the men down yet another passage, hiding along the way behind another cabinet, a huge vase and finally a life-sized statue of a very tall woman. The statue wore an elaborate headdress in the shape of an upside-down V and a very wide gown, which made a perfect hiding place. Lucy crouched down behind the statue and waited to see what happened next.

Lord Grave and Sir Percy stood facing a door at the end of the passageway.

"Shall we go in?" Lord Percy said.

"Of course. Let me fetch the key from my great-grandmother."

Great-grandmother? Surely Lord Grave was far too old to have a great-grandmother? And wouldn't Lucy have met her by now if she lived at Grave Hall? So where was she?

A few seconds later, Lucy discovered the answer to

all these questions. Lord Grave turned away from the door and headed straight towards the statue. Lucy squashed herself down as small as she could under the cover of Lord Grave's great-grandmother's stone skirts. She didn't dare risk peering round the statue, so she couldn't see what Lord Grave was doing. But she could hear. And what she heard was a giggle. A woman's giggle.

There was a grating noise and Lord Grave's great-grandmother's stone arm began to move. Lucy heard a small *chink*. Then Lord Grave stepped away from the statue. There was now a key in his hand, which he used to open the door to the room opposite. He and Lord Percy went inside.

Lucy crept out from behind the statue and eyeballed it suspiciously. It looked stony and unmoving, as a statue should. But Lucy was sure it had somehow given Lord Grave the key to the door.

She decided to find a new hiding place where she could have a better view of what was happening. She chose one of the giant vases further up the passageway and then waited to see what Lord Grave did when he came out of the room.

"Are you satisfied that there remains no chance of escape from the Room of Curiosities?" Lord Grave said, as he and Lord Percy finally emerged some minutes later.

"Yes. Of course. Thank you," Lord Percy smiled rather stiffly.

No chance of escape? Could that mean Eddie Robinson was imprisoned in what Lord Grave had called the Room of Curiosities? And were the other missing children there too?

Lucy watched closely as Lord Grave tickled his great-grandmother under her stone chin (or chins; she had several of them). As before, the statue giggled then, Lucy saw, held out her hand. Lord Grave dropped the key to the mysterious room into her upturned palm, which she slipped into a stone bag tied at her waist before freezing into her former position.

As soon as Lord Grave and Lord Percy were out of sight, Lucy crept out from behind the vase and over to the statue. She stared up into its lifeless eyes.

Feeling rather foolish and scared all at the same time, Lucy tickled Lord Grave's great-grandmother under her chins.

The statue twitched into life, smiled and began to giggle. It was all rather disturbing and Lucy couldn't help flinching away. But she pulled herself together and stretched out her hand expectantly. As she'd hoped, Lord Grave's great-grandmother dropped the key into her palm. Now to find out what was inside the Room of Curiosities.

She paused for a second. What would she find? Caged children? Something worse? Lucy swallowed her fear, took a deep breath and opened the door.

When she stepped over the threshold, she found herself in a large windowless room full of marble plinths with not a stolen child in sight. Half relieved and half disappointed, she began examining the plinths more closely. A glass dome sat on each of them, and beneath each glass was a curiosity. There was a china doll under one. It had eyes that seemed to follow Lucy. Another held a small human-like figure, made out of twigs.

Perhaps it was a trick of the light, but as she stared Lucy was sure she saw the stick figure move its limbs. She jerked back in surprise, steadying herself against the glass case behind her which, she realised, held a black metal raven with spiky feathers, its beak open in mid caw.

Seized with inquisitiveness, Lucy decided to take a closer look. As her fingertips touched the bird's glass dome a tingling began in her hand and ran all along her arm to her elbow. At the same time, the lamps burning on the walls blazed more brightly for a few seconds. How strange.

Despite her growing unease, Lucy couldn't waste the opportunity to investigate. She removed the dome before hesitantly stroking the bird's feathers. They were cold. Then, to Lucy's horror, the raven began to *move*. It whirred and shuddered and trembled before snapping its beak open and closed.

"At last!" it said, cocking its head and staring at Lucy. Its eyes were like two fresh drops of blood. "And where exactly did you come from?"

CHAPTER EIGHT

THE RAVEN

Lucy's brain began shouting furiously at her.

It's alive! Talking in a man's voice! Get away from it!

"Oh, come now, you're not afraid, are you?" said the raven. He hopped down from the plinth, and began stumping towards Lucy.

Click, click, click went his claws against the pink marble floor. Lucy stepped backwards.

"It's not natural," she whispered.

"Not natural?" cawed the raven. "I'm so very glad you told me. I don't think I ever received that particular epistle."

The raven's sarcasm made Lucy bristle with annoyance. But now wasn't the time to argue. Now was the time to get out of here. This was one unearthly event too many.

"Going to make a run for it?" said the raven. "Don't. Grave, Percy and the other fools are hanging around on the landing. They'll spot you. And if they guess you've been in here, well . . . that could be fatal. For you."

Lucy wasn't at all sure she should trust this peculiar bird. But if he was right, and Lord Grave and his guests were nearby, she couldn't leave yet.

Keeping a sensible distance from the raven, Lucy asked, "So you know Lord Grave and those other people?"

"Oh, I know them all right. Criminals." The bird watched Lucy carefully as he spoke.

I knew it, Lucy thought. *I knew there was something bad going on here.* "What have they done exactly?"

"Terrible things. Things that any decent, upstanding person deplores," the raven said. His voice grew louder and more indignant with every word.

"*Shh*," Lucy said, "someone might hear you!"

"It's very difficult not to get angry," the raven said. But he lowered his voice all the same. "What Grave's done to me and other magicians like me. The way he's used magic to—"

"Magicians?" Lucy said. "Magic?"

The raven must have seen the doubtful look on Lucy's face. The look that said *what is all this poppycock*? He sighed and shrugged his wings squeakily. "I sense disbelief on your part. Tell me, does Grave still perform that ridiculous charade with the statue of his great-grandmother?"

Lucy nodded.

"So, you've seen a statue come to life. You're talking to a clockwork raven. What else would you call such things? Everyday occurrences?"

"I suppose you have a point," Lucy said grudgingly, thinking again of her card, the strange arrival of Lord Grave's guests and the everlasting food served at last night's dinner party. "But what happened to you? Why were you in that glass case? Do you have a name?"

"Alas, I cannot tell you." The raven stretched one of his wings out dramatically.

"Why?"

"Alas, I cannot tell you that either." He stretched his other wing out and drooped his head.

"You must know!"

"Yes."

"But you can't tell me?"

"No. You could try guessing."

"Guessing what?"

The raven looked up. "Yes. And no."

"Yes and no what?"

"Do try and use your brain."

"What? Oh, wait. Maybe it's like one of those guessing games. I ask you a question and you say yes or no? Is that how it works?"

"Yes."

"So are you really a raven?"

"No."

"Are you a human? A man? A magician?"

"Yes."

"And Lord Grave magicianed you, or whatever you call it."

"Yes. Enchanted. At least get the terminology right."

"And part of the enchantment is not being able to tell anyone what's happened to you? Or why? So you're trapped here?"

"Yes, trapped." The raven spoke quietly now and hung his metal head.

"I'm trapped here too," Lucy replied sadly.

"In that case perhaps we can aid each other, Lucy." The raven cocked his head, beady eyes intense now. "You free me from this enchantment, and then I can help you escape. It must be dreadful to have been taken from your parents."

Lucy stared at the raven. "How do you know about that? And how do you know my name?"

"Grave and Percy were discussing you and how they stole you. You see, they and the rest of their cronies are—"

The raven began to cough. Then he began to choke as

though he'd swallowed something and it had gone down the wrong way. It sounded like a knife being sharpened on a stone. Lucy slapped him on his metal back.

"Thank you," said the raven, when he'd recovered. "That's what happens when I try to speak about Grave's crimes."

"You were going to say Lord Grave and his horrible friends are stealing children, weren't you?" Lucy said, half frightened at the thought of Lord Grave really being a child snatcher and half excited because what she'd suspected had turned out to be true.

The raven goggled at Lucy. "Most impressive. How did you find out?"

Lucy explained about the reports in the *Penny Dreadful* and the sinister conversation she'd overheard at last night's dinner party.

"But what do they do with the stolen children? And who is Ma'am? They kept talking about her. Is she someone very wicked?" Lucy asked. "Oh, but you can't tell me, can you? Could I guess, then you say yes or no like before? That way you wouldn't choke again."

The raven shook his head. "If you had a hundred

years, a thousand years, you would never be able to guess. You are in great danger. But there may be a way out. If you free me, I can help you."

"Free you? How?"

"There is bound to be something in this house that could do the job. But—"

"You can't tell me what kind of thing because of the enchantment?"

The raven cocked its head again and was silent for a moment. Then he sighed and said, "Sadly, that is correct. But I am sure a clever child like you can find out."

"Then we can both be free? And what about the other children? Could we help them? Or is it," Lucy shivered, then whispered, "*too late?*"

"We might be able to get to them in time. Now, I think it's finally safe for you to leave. Put me back where you found me. Trust no one. Keep your eyes open for a magical object that could help me."

"Don't you mean us?"

"Of course. Us. Then come back and we'll talk some more."

CHAPTER NINE

THE LIBRARY WITHOUT BOOKS

That night, Lucy lay wide awake yet again, staring at the dark ceiling, her mind and stomach churning. In the next bed, Becky smacked her lips in her sleep, slurping wetly. Smell was curled up at Becky's feet, snoring.

The more Lucy turned everything over in her mind, the more certain she became that her only option was to trust the raven. What other choice was there? Even if she managed to escape Grave Hall by herself and then went to the police and told them what she knew about the missing children, they probably wouldn't believe her. Lord Grave was a rich and powerful man and she was just an ordinary girl. And she had no actual solid proof of his dreadful deeds yet. It was up to her to save herself – again – and the other stolen children. But she could only do it with the raven's help.

So she decided to do what the raven had asked – look for a magical object with the power to break the enchantment he was under. But she didn't even know what she was looking for.

"I need to learn how magic works," Lucy said softly to herself. If she could do that, she might be able to work out what sort of object she needed to find.

"Ah," said a voice.

Lucy sat up, her heart thudding. She slipped out of bed and scrabbled around to light the candle next to her bed.

"Who's there?" she whispered.

"Us. We're over here," the voice replied.

It seemed to be coming from the fireplace. Perhaps one of the chimney-sweep boys was wedged up the chimney. Lucy knelt down on the floor in front of the fireplace and held up her candle.

"Are you stuck?" she called softly, not wanting to wake Becky and Smell.

"Stuck? Of course not."

Lucy nearly dropped her candle in shock. The voice wasn't coming from up the chimney. It was coming from one of the men pictured in the tiles round the fireplace, the one smoking a long pipe. Lucy could smell the smoke puffing out of it. She held her candle higher in order to see better. In the flickering light that cast long shadows across the ceiling, she saw the pipe man stroll forward. There was a faint *pop* as he left his tiles. He walked swiftly across the hearth, his ceramic feet making light tapping noises on the ground, pipe smoke drifting behind him. When he reached the other side of the fireplace, he stepped into the tiles there, which showed another man sitting reading a book. The book man got to his feet. He and the pipe man turned to face Lucy.

"We're Turner and Paige. I'm Mr Turner," said the man with the pipe. "And this is Mr Paige." Mr Paige didn't speak, but nodded shyly at Lucy. "If you need to learn about something, we're the gentlemen to help. We're librarians."

"Librarians?"

"Yes, we take care of Lord Grave's library."

Hope fluttered in Lucy's stomach. This could be the first step towards finding the magical object she needed in order to free the raven and get his help. "Can I visit it?"

Mr Turner puffed thoughtfully on his pipe. "What do you think, Mr Paige?"

Mr Paige nodded.

"That's decided then. Take my hand, miss. You can only visit the library if accompanied by us or Lord Grave."

Lucy reached out and took Mr Turner's hand between her thumb and forefinger. It was cool and smooth, like the handle of a cup. She was careful not to squeeze too hard as she didn't want to crack anything.

At first, nothing happened.

But then it was as though a heavy weight was squashing her head down into her neck, her neck into her stomach and her stomach into her feet. Lucy closed her eyes, certain they were about to burst out of her head and roll into the hearth like two gobstoppers.

At that moment, the just-about-to-burst feeling faded. Lucy opened her eyes and realised with a jolt that her gaze was now on a level with Mr Turner's. Cold began creeping up her arm and across her whole body. Lucy watched, half fascinated, half terrified, as her skin changed from its normal soft warmth, turning to something cold and hard, like the ceramic Turner and Paige were made of.

Everything went dark for a few seconds. Then Lucy found herself standing in another hearth, this time in a room far grander than the humble bedroom she shared with Becky. It had a high domed ceiling, painted midnight blue with gold stars sprinkled across it.

Lucy tried to step forward, but found she was

unable to move. She realised that she was part of the tiles surrounding the fireplace.

"Don't worry, miss," said Mr Turner, who was next to her in the tiles. "We're not finished yet. This next part won't hurt, but you may find it a smidge uncomfortable."

'A smidge uncomfortable' turned out to feel like being put through the wringer Lucy and Violet had used the day before to squeeze the water out of the wet washing. But at last, she was her normal-sized flesh-and-blood self again, and was able to move. Turner and Paige were no longer made of ceramic either; they had turned into full-size human men. The three of them stepped out of the rather crowded hearth.

"Welcome to Lord Grave's library." Mr Turner bowed extravagantly.

"Can I open a window for a minute? I feel a bit hot," Lucy said, quickly. She didn't feel hot at all, but she wanted to see exactly where she was in case she needed to make a quick exit.

Mr Turner nodded. "Of course."

She thrust aside the blue velvet curtains and opened one of the coloured glass windows. It was night outside. But the full moon gave enough light to see the thick ivy that grew from the ground below, past the library windows and on up to the top of the house.

"I don't understand," said Lucy, turning back to Turner and Paige. "We're still in Grave Hall, aren't we? Why did we have to go through the fireplace like that?"

"The entrance is hidden to protect his Lordship's valuable collection. He even changes the way in occasionally. Until recently, the entrance was the Grecian urn outside one of the guest bedrooms. We rather enjoyed being frolicking figures on there. Although we kept falling out with the Minotaur. He could be very bull-headed," said Mr Turner.

"But it's silly. If someone wanted to break in, they could just get a ladder or climb the ivy and come through that window!"

Mr Turner smiled. "There are measures in place to prevent that. Secret, of course."

Lucy gazed around the huge room. There were comfy-looking leather chairs and sofas scattered about. But there was only one shelf in the whole place. It was high up on the wall and held four books, one silver-coloured, one gold, one copper and one black. There was a tiny door underneath the shelf, set into the skirting board. A mouse-sized door.

"How can this be a library? There's only four books. Where are the rest?"

"There have been one or two attempted burglaries in recent years. So Lord Grave decided that Mr Paige should become the library." Mr Turner pointed his pipe at Mr Paige. "He holds all the books in his head. Much harder for rivals to steal them that way."

"How can anyone read the books if they're in his head?" Lucy snapped. It seemed she'd been through all the squashing and bursting and wringing for nothing. She was sorely tempted to grab Mr Turner's stupid pipe and shove it somewhere 'a smidge uncomfortable'. But the two tile men seemed unperturbed by her irritation.

"Shall we demonstrate, Mr Paige?"

Mr Paige gave his usual silent nod.

Mr Turner began shifting leather chairs around until three of them faced the wall with the shelf and the miniscule door beneath it. When everyone was seated, Mr Turner said, "Look at the door, miss. Concentrate on what it is you need to learn about and then say it aloud."

Lucy did as he said – she thought hard about wanting to learn how magic worked. Then she said it aloud.

To her astonishment the mouse-sized door began to grow, becoming:

Smell-sized;

Dog-sized;

Bathsheba-sized; and finally . . .

Lucy-sized.

Once it had stopped growing, the door creaked and groaned before sprouting a brass handle, a lock and a key.

"You need to go through the door and into the Reading Room. You must go through it alone, but you won't be alone on the other side of it," said Mr Turner.

Lucy walked towards the door. Then stopped. Anything could be on the other side, waiting to keep her company. And what if she couldn't get out again? She looked over her shoulder at Turner and Paige.

"Trust me, miss, you'll come to no harm," Mr Turner said.

Should she believe Mr Turner? She wasn't even sure what he was. A magician? Or some sort of strange being conjured into existence by Lord Grave? But she had to take the chance. Learning how magic worked would help her understand the sort of object she should look for in order to free the raven and herself.

Lucy grasped the doorknob. It felt like it should, metallic and slightly cold. She put her ear to the door, but all she could hear was her own breathing and pounding heart.

"Unlock it, miss."

She turned the key and then the doorknob. The door squeaked open. Lucy looked over her shoulder again at Turner and Paige before stepping over the threshold into the darkness beyond.

CHAPTER TEN

TONGUE-TIED

*B*ang!

The door slammed shut behind Lucy, leaving her in darkness so deep and black that it seemed to press against her. She was fighting down a scream when one by one seven small candles set in curly metal wall-holders flickered into life.

Beneath each candle stood a Mr Paige.

Bewildered, Lucy looked back at the door she'd come through. It was still firmly shut.

The Mr Paiges smiled. "Don't be afraid. Imparting knowledge can be tiring; spreading the load helps," they said together. "What would you like to know?"

"How does magic work exactly?" Lucy asked.

"Much depends on the skill of the magician."

"You mean whether they're good at magic or not?"

"Not quite. Most magicians have one or two particular abilities; a few may have more, although that is very unusual. The magic a magician can perform will depend on the skills they possess."

"I see." Lucy pretended to study her fingernails. "And can *things* be magical? Objects?"

"Yes, there are some who are able to imbue inanimate objects with magic."

"And how would a person know if an . . . inanimate object was imbued with magic?"

"Oh, that's very complicated. First, it would depend on whether a person could see magic. Non-magicians can't usually detect magic, although some may glimpse magic at the periphery of their consciousness."

Lucy frowned. "Pardon?"

The Mr Paiges smiled. "It means ordinary people sometimes see magic happening out of the corner of their eye."

Lucy opened her mouth to ask a million more questions. But the candles in their wall holders began to burn low and the Mr Paiges were fading too.

"This is as much as we can tell you today. We have to be careful. This is all very new to you. Too much information might make your brain explode with the strain. That would be rather messy," Mr Paige said, his voice growing fainter and fainter.

"No, please. I need to know more, much more! I can see you and you're magical, aren't you? All this is magical. But I'm seeing it right in front of me, not out of the corner of my eye. Why?"

It was too late. All the candles guttered out and the Mr Paiges vanished. The dark pressed around Lucy again. She felt dizzy and sick. When she turned to go back through the door she couldn't find it. Confused and frightened, she stumbled around, banging into things that it was too dark to see.

Something snuffled and gurgled.

Lucy backed away from the noise, wondering what horrible monster was lurking in the dark with her. She tripped over something and crashed to the floor.

The snuffling and gurgling stopped and a peeved voice said, "For pity's sake, Goodly, some of us are trying to sleep, you know."

The next day, which was a Sunday, when Lucy had fulfilled her animal duties and eaten lunch with the other servants, she found she had some unexpected free time. Lord Grave was out and everyone else was occupied. Mrs Crawley was having an afternoon nap. Violet and Vonk were trimming the animal-shaped topiary (Violet was wearing one of Vonk's spare gardening hats). Becky was deep in the latest edition of the *Penny*.

Lucy kept wondering whether any of her fellow servants knew what was going on. But she had no way of telling and so decided it was safest to keep her suspicions to herself for now.

She decided to take the opportunity to do some detective work. Although she knew a little more about magic, thanks to her library trip, she was still no wiser as to the magical object the Raven wanted her to find. But she could at least do her best to investigate the mystery of the missing children. Perhaps she could find evidence of Lord Grave's involvement and what he and Ma'am were doing with the children they stole. Then she could go to the police once she had escaped from her predicament and report what she knew.

She started her investigations by 'borrowing' back copies of the *Penny Dreadful*, which Becky kept under her bed. Lucy read every single article she could find about the disappearances. And it wasn't long before she noted that several of the reports mentioned that a black carriage had been seen near the scene of many of the crimes.

Although this ruled out Lord Grave's carriage, which was a silvery-grey colour, – what about Lady Sibyl's black carriage? The articles didn't mention flying horses, of course, but perhaps Lady Sibyl had been using normal horses at the time. That made sense. A child snatcher wouldn't want to draw attention to themselves.

Luckily for Lucy, although Lord Percy and the Beguildy twins had left Grave Hall that morning, Lady Sibyl was staying an extra night. So Lucy hurried down to the carriage house, which was next to the stables. She checked to make sure none of the coachmen were around and then sneaked inside.

Lady Sybil's black carriage was parked next to Lord Grave's. Lucy walked slowly around it. Lady Sibyl's coachman must have cleaned it recently because it gleamed and the wheels were mud-free.

Perhaps an attempt to remove any incriminating evidence?

Interesting.

Lucy tried one of the doors, expecting it to be locked. But it opened, so she climbed in. The leather seats smelled of polish and everything was as spotless inside as out. Not a clue to be seen. She was about to climb out again when she noticed a small corner of white poking out from between the rear-seat cushions. Lucy pulled it out. It was a cotton handkerchief with the initials *C. S.* embroidered in pink silk on one of the corners.

At first, Lucy decided that the handkerchief was probably just one of Lady Sibyl's. Even though the initials weren't quite right, it could be that Sibyl wasn't Lady Sibyl's first name. Sometimes people preferred to use their middle or last name instead of their first name, didn't they? She could be called something like Catherine Sibyl.

Feeling rather disappointed, Lucy was about to shove the handkerchief back where she found it, when she remembered something – the name of one of the missing children she'd read about in the *Penny*.

Claire Small.

Lucy excitedly examined the handkerchief more closely. It was made of plain cotton. No lace. Nothing fancy apart from the embroidered initials. Not the sort of handkerchief a wealthy and fashionable aristocrat would bother with. Lucy carefully folded the handkerchief and put it in her jacket pocket before climbing back out of the carriage. She was eager to visit the raven again and share this clue with him.

But someone was waiting for her at the door to the carriage house.

Or rather two someones.

One was a giraffe. The other was a small, furry, long-nosed animal of a kind Lucy had never seen before.

There shouldn't be too much to fear from a giraffe, Lucy told herself. Being a vegetarian animal, it wasn't likely to eat her. And the giraffe's companion didn't seem exactly menacing. In fact, it was rather cute.

Lucy decided to take the offensive.

"What are you doing here?" she said in a firm voice. "Have you escaped from the wildlife park? Naughty things. You should get back there right away! Shoo! Be off with you!"

Lucy waved her arms about.

The two animals ignored her. The giraffe glanced down at the long-nosed creature and the long-nosed creature looked up at the giraffe.

The giraffe's left ear twitched.

The long-nosed creature scampered towards

Lucy. She tried to dodge out of its path, but she was too slow. An impossibly long tongue shot out of the creature's narrow snout and wrapped itself round Lucy's ankle, bringing her crashing to the floor of the carriage house. With Lucy incapacitated, the giraffe lolloped over to her, bent its never-ending neck, and began worrying at Lucy's pocket. The pocket tore and the giraffe snatched the handkerchief.

"Please. Please give it back to me. You don't understand!" Lucy tried to stand, but the tongue remained firmly entwined round her ankle.

The giraffe turned and headed out of the carriage house, carrying the handkerchief in its mouth. The long-nosed creature reclaimed its tongue from Lucy's ankle and scuttled off too, making a squeaking noise as it went, almost as though it was giggling.

CHAPTER ELEVEN

THE SMELL OF A SPY

Lucy's mind churned all through supper. She barely noticed what she was eating, much to Mrs Crawley's disappointment.

"No thoughts on my cabbage, marmalade and pickled onion casserole?" she asked sadly.

"Um, it was very . . . piquant," Lucy said.

As Lord Grave had decided to dine out with Lady Sibyl, there was less work that evening than usual. Lucy grabbed the chance to sneak away and pay another visit to the raven to report her findings. But she'd just set off down the east wing corridor towards the Room of Curiosities when a pungent whiff made her eyes water. She turned round. Smell was ambling along behind her.

"Why are you following me? Go away!" she said, clapping her hands.

Smell sat down and began washing one of his back legs. Lucy paused. She really didn't want the cat to see what she was up to. It seemed ridiculous, but it felt almost as if he was spying on her. Perhaps she was wrong about the giraffe and its friend being harmless? Perhaps all the animals here were spies, absurd as that seemed.

Lucy dug into her apron pocket and found a piece of cake she'd reluctantly agreed to taste-test yesterday for Mrs Crawley. Lemon and beef sponge with curried icing. Lucy had only pretended to eat and enjoy it before slipping it into her pocket. She'd meant to throw it away later, but then had forgotten all about it. Until now. The cake was more doughy than spongy, so she rolled it into a ball and sent it spinning across the floor. It trundled under a cabinet. Smell spotted the not-so-delicious morsel immediately, scooted over to the cabinet and began trying to squeeze his head underneath it. When he found his head wouldn't fit, he tried his paw instead. Lucy ran off while he wasn't looking, hastily tickled Lord Grave's great-grandmother's chins and once again let herself into the Room of Curiosities.

"Have you found a magical object?" the raven said, once she had brought him to life again.

"How lovely to see you too. No, not yet. I don't even know what I'm looking for and you can't tell me. But I have found a few things out as well as something to prove Lord Grave and his friends are guilty." She explained about the library, and about Turner and Paige, and about the handkerchief she'd found.

"Do you have the handkerchief?" the raven asked anxiously.

"No. I . . . er . . . lost it," Lucy said, too embarrassed to admit that a giraffe and a creature with a talented tongue had managed to outwit her.

"And what about Ma'am? Have you identified her yet?" the raven said, beginning to sound anxious.

"No," Lucy said, feeling rather inadequate.

The raven clicked his beak impatiently. "None of this is very helpful. And it's most disappointing you haven't found an object that could help us. I thought you were a moderately bright young person."

Lucy's cheeks grew warm. "Oh well. Maybe I'll just put you back in your case then. If you're so very marvellous I'm sure you can get yourself out of the mess you're in."

The raven hastily backtracked. "My apologies. All this is very new to you. I shouldn't expect too much too soon. After all, you've only experienced magic in the last few days."

"Actually, you're very wrong about that," Lucy said, enjoying the look of surprise on the raven's face. At least she thought he looked surprised. His beak was certainly hanging open. She told the raven about the card she'd stolen from Lady Red and what it could do. When she got to the part about Mrs Milligan's Gambling Den and Lord Grave taking her from her parents, her throat went tight and she had to stop speaking.

"Well, come on, tell me more. The woman you stole the card from. What did she look like?"

"She had long shiny red hair. She was beautiful. But her eyes . . ."

"What about them?"

"Just for a few seconds, it was as though they were made of fire. Like Catherine wheels." Lucy shuddered at the memory.

"Amethyst," the raven muttered.

"No, orangey-red, like fire. Isn't amethyst more of a purple colour?"

"Yes, I know!" the raven snapped.

"Well, pardon me! Maybe you should find someone else to help you after all. I don't have to put up with this, you know."

"I'm sorry, Lucy. It's the strain. Can you imagine what it's been like for me, imprisoned in this contraption for years on end? It would make anyone waspish. Now let's take stock," the raven said, suddenly sounding a lot more cheerful. "You have access to Grave's library. That's good. In fact . . . in fact I think you may have found an object to help us after all!"

"I have? And it'll help the other children too?" Lucy said eagerly.

"Naturally. Kill three birds with one stone, as they say," the raven cawed at his own joke.

Lucy smiled politely, silently urging him to get on with it.

"Alas, I cannot tell you what that object is," the raven said, sounding somewhat deflated again.

Lucy huffed in exasperation and kicked the side of the raven's plinth. A cloud of dust rose up, making her cough. She felt most dejected. But the raven began hopping about excitedly.

"Lucy, you're a genius!" he cried, and hopped off the plinth into the patch of dust. He began writing something in it with his beak.

Find the Wish Book.

Lucy stared at what the raven had written.

"You can read, I take it?" the raven snapped, dust drifting from his beak.

"Yes, of course I can! But there aren't any actual books in the library. I told you that. All the books are inside Mr Paige's head." Lucy tapped her own skull to illustrate, in case the raven hadn't properly understood.

"No books at all? Think! Think!"

Lucy thought. And then remembered. "There were some books on a shelf. Maybe four. They were made of metal, I think. Is the Wish Book one of them?"

"Yes!"

"So I need to steal it? But how?" Lucy asked.

"I'm sure you'll think of something," said the raven.

CHAPTER TWELVE

ᗴᑎOᑌGᕼ ᓰᔕ ᗴᑎOᑌGᕼ

A nd the very next day, when she was baking inside her armour while sweeping up Bathsheba's dirty straw (the panther was busy tearing away at several roast chickens Lucy had given her), she did think of something. What she thought of was that she'd had enough.

Enough of the weird goings-on at Grave Hall.

Enough of Becky Bone calling her names.

Enough of the raven bossing her around.

Enough of Lord Grave and his threats.

Enough of worrying about her parents and waiting for them to find a way to rescue her.

And definitely enough of having to muck out Bathsheba's hut while dressed in a suit of armour.

Surely she could find a way of escaping on her own without having to steal the Wish Book? And once she did, she could get help for the stolen children and the raven too. There was a risk that Lord Grave might follow up on his threat to report her for cheating at cards. But would he really risk drawing attention to himself by kicking up trouble? Someone might discover *his* dastardly crimes.

Lucy swept Bathsheba's straw more furiously, trying to think it all out. Bathsheba, who was in a friendly mood today, batted at Lucy's broom in a manner more suited to a kitten than a potentially lethal panther.

"Oh, come on, get out of the way!" Lucy gently shoved Bathsheba aside. Bathsheba not so gently nipped Lucy's fingers, but the gauntlets Lucy wore as part of her armour prevented any real damage.

Armour.

Why hadn't she thought of it before?

She could go now. Right at this very moment. Run through the wildlife park to the gates she'd come through in Lord Grave's carriage that first day. She was sure she'd be able to climb over them. And her armour would protect her from attack by Bathsheba or any of the other animals.

She flung aside her broom and ran out of the hut. And kept running. Or rather kept waddling. Her armour was heavy, a little rusty and not conducive to moving at speed. She rattled and squeaked past the lake, where one of the elephants was enjoying a drink. The elephant turned at the sound of Lucy's armour. It had very long and very sharp tusks.

Nothing to worry about, elephants are harmless unless you get in the way of their feet, Lucy told herself and waddled on. But she quickly found she couldn't waddle any further. Because the elephant was standing in front of her, like a grey, living mountain. How had it moved so quickly?

Lucy squinted up at the elephant.

The elephant glared down at Lucy.

Its tusks glinted in the sunlight.

"Um, don't worry. No need to move – I'll go around you," Lucy said.

She moved to her left.

So did the elephant.

She moved to her right.

So did the elephant.

Lucy and the elephant repeated this dance several times. Then the elephant seemed to get bored. It snorted, bent its great grey head and then hooked one of its tusks through the gap in Lucy's armour where the sleeve was attached to the shoulder plate.

The elephant lifted Lucy high into the air. Lucy squealed and squirmed but the elephant took no notice. Ears and trunk flapping, it thundered back the way Lucy had come. It reached the iron fence, which separated the animals from the rest of Grave Hall, and lowered her over it, dropping her the last few feet. Lucy landed with a thud that rattled her armour and her teeth. The armour protected her from breaking any bones, but the fall still hurt. She lay on

the ground, trying not to cry from pain, humiliation and utter despair. Now there could be no doubting that she was being thwarted by Grave Hall's animal residents. That elephant had deliberately foiled her escape attempt. It was impossible, but the impossible seemed to happen on a daily basis at Grave Hall.

When she'd recovered a little, Lucy limped back towards the house, comforting herself with the thought that at least no one had witnessed her embarrassing defeat. When she reached the kitchen garden, she found Mrs Crawley there, sitting in a striped deckchair, drinking out of a large tankard. Her frock was hoisted up to her knees, showing her hairy legs. She was wearing a pair of sandals, which her equally hairy toes poked out of. Whatever was in the tankard smelled almost as bad as Smell had when he'd overindulged on devilled kidneys a few days ago.

"Ah, Lucy!" she said. "Would you like a sip?"

"No, thanks. What is it, liquidised dung or something?"

Mrs Crawley tittered. "It's the first batch of my home-brewed ale. I admit it has a certain pungency to it. Probably due to a small sprinkling of my Extra Violent Mustard Mix that I added during the brewing process. I thought I'd have a quick taste to check if it's ready and gather my strength before starting on the dinner. I'll need some help as little Violet hasn't turned up for work today. Very unlike her. She must be ill. Would you mind serving his Lordship's afternoon tea once you've taken your armour off? Here, let me give you a hand."

As Mrs Crawley began unbuckling the armour, Lucy wondered desperately if the housekeeper-cum-cook knew what was really going on at Grave Hall? Surely not? She so wanted to confide in Mrs Crawley. But perhaps it would be too risky. Lucy reluctantly decided that her best bet was to bide her time.

A quarter of an hour later, Lucy was standing outside Lord Grave's study holding a tray of tea things. She was about to knock when she heard raised voices.

"'Ow many more children is it going to take, Grave? You need to do something," said a gruff voice.

Lucy trembled. The cup on her tray rattled against the teapot.

"I don't have to do anything," Lord Grave snapped.

"You blooming well do. Ma'am thinks that you—"

"I don't need to be told what Ma'am does or doesn't think! Concentrate on what you're supposed to be doing, but do it better. Or *I* might have a quiet word with Ma'am about *you*. Stop getting distracted."

"Can't 'elp it. It's my nature now."

"A feeble excuse. I think—"

Crash!

Lucy had been so intent on listening to this tense exchange between Lord Grave and what must be one of the dreaded Ma'am's henchmen that she'd let her tray tilt and the teacup had smashed to the floor.

Lord Grave flung open the door, frowning bushily.

"I-I was bringing you your tea," said Lucy.

"Go in, put it on the table."

"But I broke the cup."

"Leave it, I'll deal with it." Lord Grave bent down and began picking up the shards of china.

Lucy stepped into the drawing room.

There was no one else there.

She busied herself setting out the teapot and the milk jug, looking around to see if there was someone hiding under the table or behind the sofa. But she couldn't see anyone. There was a whiff though. A whiff that made her wrinkle her nose in disgust.

"Violet usually brings me my tea. Where is she?" Lord Grave demanded, placing the teacup she had dropped on to the table.

The teacup was whole again.

Lucy stared at the cup and then up at Lord Grave.

"She's ill, we think," she muttered.

"You think? What's wrong with her?"

"I don't know."

"She hasn't sent a message?"

"No."

"I see. Did you hurt yourself?" he said.

"When the cup broke? No, it—"

"No. I meant with Elvira. I heard you had an encounter with her."

Lucy put her hand to her mouth. No one else had seen what happened. So it was true. The animals were acting against her, spying on her and somehow reporting back to Lord Grave.

"Yes. I know everything that happens in this house. And I know—" He paused.

Lucy waited for him to say he knew about everything else she'd been up to. Visiting the library, and the raven. Her investigations into Lady Sibyl's carriage.

"I know you don't want to be here, Lucy. That's natural. I promise all of this will make sense soon."

"Why can't it make sense now?"

Lord Grave didn't reply, but strode over to the door and opened it. His stern expression told her that their not-so-cosy chat was over. Lucy turned and left the room. When Lord Grave had closed the door behind her, she leaned against the wall. Once her heart had stopped thumping quite so hard and her legs were less wobbly, she walked slowly back to the kitchen.

What did Lord Grave mean by *all of this will make sense soon*? Would that be when he was using her for whatever horrific purpose he and Ma'am had in mind? And that would probably be sooner rather than later now that Lord Grave knew what she'd been up to and was no doubt suspicious of her. Lucy couldn't escape on her own; her disastrous attempt had proved that. And she had no idea how she was going to get to the Wish Book without Lord Grave's network of spies detecting her.

Things really can't get any worse, she thought.

But then they did.

TRAGEDY AT GRAVE HALL!

THE *PENNY DREADFUL* has tirelessly reported the disturbing instances of children going missing last year. A full list of the missing can be found on page two.

Now, once again, the *Penny* is the first to regretfully inform its loyal readers that yet another child has vanished. Violet Worthington was taken from Grave Village on Monday.

ZOMBIES!

Witnesses reported seeing the child climb into a mysterious black carriage.

The unfortunate Violet was employed as a part-time scullery maid at Grave Hall.

Grave Hall has been tainted with tragedy before. Lady Grave succumbed to scarlet fever there eight years ago. And Lord Albert Grave, the only child of Lord Grave, died five years ago under mysterious circumstances at the tender age of seven.

Our intrepid reporter Slimeous Osburn attempted to visit Grave Hall and interview his Lordship about the disappearance of Violet Worthington, but a ferocious panther and a deranged elephant chased him off.

The *Penny* is convinced that all the missing children cases are linked in some way. However, now Sir Absalom Balderdash's flesh-eating zombie theory has been thoroughly discredited, it is difficult to establish what this link might be.

CHAPTER THIRTEEN

THE EYES OF CARUTHERS

It had been two days since Violet had gone missing. All the Grave Hall servants were gathered round the kitchen table. Except for Mrs Crawley, who was attempting a new recipe to distract herself. She had her back to everyone as she stirred a pot on the kitchen range, but Lucy could see the housekeeper-cum-cook's shoulders shaking as she stifled a sob.

"His Lordship's having a meeting now with Lady Sibyl and the rest of . . . his friends. They're going to help organise a search. Poor little Violet." Vonk said. He took out a large striped handkerchief and blew his nose.

"Poor little milksop," agreed Becky, stroking Smell, who was curled up on her lap. She sounded almost sad.

As for Lucy, she said nothing. Fury boiled inside her as she reread the names of the missing children listed in the *Penny*. Couldn't any of Lord Grave's household see what was happening? It was obvious to Lucy that Lord Grave had taken Violet. It was ruthlessly clever of him. No one would suspect him of kidnapping his own scullery maid.

What would he do to her? Hand her over to the mysterious Ma'am? Violet with her kind heart and soft voice would have no chance of saving herself. Lucy couldn't bear to think of the terrible magic that might be practised on the poor child. Lucy looked up from the *Penny* and gazed round the table. Should she tell the other servants her suspicions? But what if one of them, or all of them, were in on it too?

After a while, Vonk got up from the table and went

into his butler's pantry, which lay just off the kitchen. When he came back, he was wearing his green floppy gardener's hat.

"I think the best thing we can do is get back to work. Mrs C, is there any chance I could snaffle a couple of pails of your latest home-brew? The one with your Extra Violent Mustard Mix added to it?"

Mrs Crawley turned from the range. Her beard stuck out in tufts, as though she'd been raking it with her fingers and her eyes were red. "Resorting to drink won't help us find Violet," she sniffled.

"I don't want to drink it! The roses have terrible greenfly and I thought a good drenching with that ale might be just the thing."

"Oh, Vonk!"

"Bernie, I'm not saying the ale isn't delicious – merely that it's multifunctional," Vonk said hastily.

Mrs Crawley brightened a little. "I'm sure I can spare some in that case."

"Thank you. Why don't you have a little nap before starting on lunch, Mrs C? You look worn out."

"I might just do that. Lucy, would you help Vonk

take a couple of pails to the potting shed?"

Lucy agreed readily, because at last a plan to successfully steal the Wish Book was forming in her mind and a visit to Vonk's potting shed could provide her with something she needed.

She and Vonk made their way outside in silence. When they were nearly at the potting shed, Lucy decided to risk some subtle questioning to find out if she could trust Vonk or not.

"Do you think Lord Grave will be able to find Violet?"

"If anyone can find her, he can," Vonk said.

"Because he's so important? And he's powerful too, isn't he? In . . . lots of different ways."

They had reached the shed by now. Vonk opened the door and ushered Lucy inside. "Yes, that's right. Now put that bucket on the work table over there," Vonk said, his back to Lucy as he took down various packages from the shelves that lined one wall.

Lucy did as he asked, then swiftly surveyed the shed. There were various gardening tools hanging from hooks on the wall opposite the shelves. While

Vonk's back was still turned, Lucy unhooked a small pair of shears.

"Do you think there's a link between Violet and the other children?" Lucy asked, when she'd safely pocketed the tool.

Vonk turned back to the bucket and began carefully pouring the contents of a bottle into it. "Ma'am—" He stopped, looking horrified. The bottle slipped from his grasp and landed in the bucket with a splash. He began fishing it out. "I mean, ma . . . many people think that is a possibility."

There was an awkward pause. Lucy's heart thudded. So Vonk was part of the kidnapping plot too! He was bound to warn Ma'am and Lord Grave that he'd slipped up. And that meant Lucy was in more immediate danger than ever.

"Well, if you don't need me for anything else, I've got some boots to see to," she said, forcing herself to sound calm, even though her insides squirmed with fear as well as disappointment at Vonk's treachery.

"That's fine. Off you go," Vonk replied in a strained voice.

"See you later then," Lucy said brightly. She left the shed as nonchalantly as she could and began strolling back to the house.

But when she was sure Vonk couldn't see her, she raced over the manicured lawns. As she ran, she noted with relief that Lord Grave, his revolting cronies and Bathsheba were down by the lake, having a pre-lunch walk. *No doubt planning their next despicable move*, Lucy thought. Which could well involve something nasty happening to Lucy herself. There was now no time to lose in putting her plan to steal the Wish Book into action. Then she could free the raven and he would help her escape. After that, she would find a way to rescue Violet and the other missing children.

Lucy whipped through the vegetable garden and into the kitchen, which was thankfully empty. Mrs Crawley must be having her nap. Lucy caught her breath for a moment. As she did so, she had a sudden thought. She rummaged through the kitchen store cupboard and grabbed a tin before creeping upstairs, heading for her room.

She paused in the hallway to check for danger.

But the house was quiet. Becky was nowhere to be seen, neither was Smell. Lucy sprinted off again and up the stairs. But in her haste, she tripped on the last stair before the first-floor landing, staggered and then fell sideways. She crashed into the cabinet she'd once hidden behind. It rocked on its spindly legs and its doors flew open. A number of wooden boxes tumbled out. Lucy picked herself up and was about to run off again when she noticed each box had a label pasted on it. She grabbed one of them. The label said *Harold Jameson*. Inside was a toy ship, with its masts broken. Lucy knelt down and opened another labelled *Deborah Jones*. A red hair ribbon lay inside, torn in half. Heart thumping, Lucy noticed that one of the boxes looked newer than the rest.

Violet Worthington!

Lucy fumbled the box open. Something green and woolly lay inside.

Caruthers.

Violet's beloved knitted frog.

Poor Caruthers looked rather mangled. Two strands of black thread hung from where his button eyes had been and a hole in his stomach was leaking sawdust.

There was something else in the box too. A note. The handwriting was cramped, untidy and very hard to read. Lucy could just about make out the words *Ma'am particularly wants to* but the rest was illegible.

This was it.

Conclusive, absolute proof that Lord Grave was responsible for the missing children together with Ma'am, who seemed to have something 'particular' in mind for poor little Violet.

Lucy was sure of only one thing.

She needed to act now and act fast. Otherwise Violet and the other children were as good as dead. And soon Lucy would be too.

CHAPTER FOURTEEN

LUCY'S EXPLODING BRAIN

ramming Caruthers into her pocket, Lucy continued dashing up the stairs, more determined than ever to steal the Wish Book, free the raven and bring Lord Grave, Ma'am and all the rest of them to justice. When she reached her room, she snatched up a cloth bag belonging to Becky and stuffed the tin she'd taken from the kitchen inside it along with a long woollen scarf she found in Becky's chest of drawers. Panting, she knelt by the fireplace. Turner and Paige were motionless on the tiles as normal.

"Psst!" Lucy hissed.

Neither of them moved.

"Oi!" Lucy said more loudly. She poked Mr Turner in the side, then did the same to Mr Paige. The tiles were cold and hard against her fingertips. Why weren't they waking up?

Lucy sat back on her heels, thinking hard. What was it she'd said when she'd first seen them come to life? It seemed like weeks had passed since then, but it was only a few days ago. Wasn't it something about wanting to learn how magic worked?

Learn.

Libraries were places of learning. Perhaps then, that was the word that woke Turner and Paige?

So she whispered, "I want to learn about . . . magicians." It seemed somewhat feeble, but right now her aim was to get inside the library and there was no time to come up with something more convincing.

After a few moments, the two men began to move in their tiles. Once again, at his invitation, she took

Mr Turner's hand and they passed through the bedroom fireplace into the library.

There above the mouse-sized door were the books, one of which could solve all her problems. If only she could grab it now! But she had to wait for the right moment. So, she reluctantly went through the palaver of watching the mouse-sized door grow to Lucy-sized before joining the seven Mr Paiges in the reading room. This time it was the Mr Paige who stood furthest to the left who spoke first.

"You want to learn about magicians?"

"Yes."

"What exactly do you want to know?"

"I . . . um . . . how does someone become a magician?"

"Magicians are born not made."

"And . . . how do magicians *do* magic, exactly? Do they cast spells?"

"There are various ways of creating magic. Spells, potions, even the power of the imagination."

"Lord Grave's a magician, isn't he?" Lucy said.

"That's correct," said Mr Paige.

"And . . . are there good magicians and evil ones?"

"Yes, that is the case," Mr Paige said slowly. He sounded wary, as though he was rather uncomfortable with the way the conversation was heading. "And on that note, I think we should stop for today."

"But I have lots more to ask!"

"As we said last time you visited, we are only allowed to tell you a small amount at each visit. Otherwise—"

"Oh, yes, my brain might explode. Ridiculous idea. As if," Lucy said and rolled her eyes.

"Not at all! It's a genuine risk!"

"But I've hardly asked you anything. I think we should go on."

"No. We really mustn't."

Lucy stamped her foot. "But you have to! I— Ow! Ow! Ow! Ow!"

"What's wrong?" the Mr Paiges cried.

Lucy collapsed to the floor. She curled herself into a little ball, clutching her head. "I think it might be too late. All this talk about magicians. It's too much to take in. I think my brain *is* going to explode.

I have a terrible headache."

The seven Mr Paiges crowded round her. They shouted for Mr Turner, who raced in, almost dashing his own brains out as the door was still Lucy-sized not Mr Turner-sized.

"Oh, Mr Paige, what's happened?"

"She says we've overfilled her brain!"

"What exactly have you been telling her? Have you overdone it?"

"Overdone it! Of course not! We hardly told her anything! We're always very careful about how much information we impart!"

"Well, you've done something to the poor child!"

The seven Mr Paiges surrounded the one Mr Turner and they all started shouting at each other. And while they bickered, snapped and argued, Lucy uncurled herself, crawled through the legs of the Mr Paiges surrounding her and sped out of the Reading Room, back into the library. Silently, she closed the door behind her and turned the key in the lock before taking it out of the keyhole and dropping it in her jacket pocket.

She leaned against the door, shaking.

"Lucy, let us out!" shouted Mr Turner. "Please, miss!"

"Will not!" Lucy shouted back.

She had to hurry. Paige and Turner were clearly magical in some way and could probably deal with a locked door. If only it was mouse-sized again. Even in their fireplace form, Turner and Paige were almost a foot high and too big to get through it. At the very least, it might slow them down.

As she was thinking this, the door wobbled.

Became Bathsheba-sized.

Dog-sized.

Smell-sized.

Mouse-sized!

Lucy watched, amazed and delighted. Locking the door must have automatically triggered its size-changing magic.

Now all she had to do was find the Wish Book and take it to the raven.

Lucy pushed one of the leather sofas against the mouse-sized door, underneath the shelf that held the metal books. This also helped to muffle Turner and Paige's shouts. The sofa had a high back and by perching on it and stretching up as high as she possibly could, Lucy's fingertips reached the edges of the books. Now she was up closer, she could see there were five of them. Four metal books, one gold, one silver, one copper, one iron, and one book that wasn't metal, but made of glassy, see-through material.

Lucy eased out the book with the iron cover. Everything inside it was black, including the pages. She shook it to see if it would do anything, tell her anything. But it remained dark and silent so she dropped it on the sofa. She pulled the gold book out next, but the pages inside were in a language she didn't understand. Lucy slung it on the sofa in disgust. How was she supposed to know which book to take when she couldn't even read their contents? She tried the silver book next. It was tucked further back on the shelf than the others and she couldn't quite reach it. She stood on her tiptoes, wobbling dangerously. Still not near enough. She gave a little leap and just managed to snatch the silver spine before losing her balance and toppling backwards. She tumbled off the sofa and on to the floor, the book falling with her. One of its pointy metal corners struck her on the head.

She lay dazed for a few seconds. When the library stopped tilting giddily around her, she sat up and grabbed the book. It was very heavy and had a sharp metallic smell. She opened it carefully and peered at the thin silver pages. Engraved on the very first page were the words:

For Wishes, Spell.

She'd found it!

But those were the only words in the whole book. The other pages had holes punched in them, just big enough for Lucy to be able to stick her finger through. The first page had one hole, the second two and so on. How could this strange object possibly free the raven? It seemed impossible to imagine.

Lucy stuck her finger through the first hole on the first page. The edges of the hole were as lethal as one of Mrs Crawley's chopping knives and she had to be careful not to slice off her fingertip.

"I wish I was at home at Leafy Ridge," she said firmly.

Nothing.

She was still in the library. No need to panic, she told herself. The raven would know how to use it. She'd better stop dithering and get it to him.

But as she was shoving the Wish Book inside the bag she'd brought with her, there was a rattling noise in the library fireplace. Lucy watched, horror-struck, as a figure appeared in the tiles. It had prominent eyebrows and a miniature black panther at its side.

CHAPTER FIFTEEN

SNIFFED OUT

Lucy dived behind the library curtains and drew them closed, leaving a small gap to peer through. Seconds later, Lord Grave and Bathsheba slid from the tiles, changing from the miniature ceramic version of themselves to full-sized flesh, blood, fur and teeth. Another figure appeared in the tiles. A figure wearing a beard, a flowery dressing gown and fluffy pink slippers.

"Where on earth have those two got to?" Lord

Grave said, frowning in his bushy-eyebrow way. "They're as bad as Smell. None of them have kept a proper eye on the girl, despite my instructions. Now look at the mess we're in."

"If only she hadn't found Caruthers," said Mrs Crawley, who was now her full six-foot-three-and-a-quarter-inches self.

Lucy almost cried out in anger and sorrow. It was horrible to discover that the housekeeper-cum-cook was in on Lord Grave's wicked activities. She must have only been pretending to be upset about Violet. Although she'd put on a most impressive act. Even now, her eyes were still rather red.

"If we don't find her, we're all at risk, Mrs C. Ma'am most of all. Imagine if Lucy goes to the authorities. Or the *Penny Dreadful*, come to think of it. If people begin nosing around . . ."

"I don't think she'll have got far," Mrs Crawley said.

Bathsheba suddenly leaped on to the sofa Lucy had shoved against the wall and started growling and clawing at the leather.

"That sofa's not usually there," Lord Grave said in a soft voice.

"And those books are normally on that shelf," Mrs Crawley replied.

Lord Grave and Mrs Crawley hurried forward and rolled the sofa away from the wall. While they were distracted, Lucy attempted to open the library window. But the handle was stiff and bound to make a harsh grating noise that would be overheard. She'd have to wait for the right opportunity.

"Turner, Paige, are you in there?" Lord Grave was shouting.

"Your Lordship, is that you?" Mr Turner replied weakly. "We're trapped! The girl, she tricked us!"

Lord Grave gave the mouse-sized door the briefest of glances. It grew Lord Grave-sized in an instant. The handle jiggled and rattled and then the door lurched open. Mr Turner and Mr Paige fell into the library, red-faced, choking, clasping their throats, as though they'd been struggling to breathe.

"The girl, your Lordship," said Mr Turner raspily. "She did this."

"The books," said Mrs Crawley. "One's missing."

Mr Turner looked at the books on the sofa and then at the shelf. "It's the Wish Book."

"Why would she take that? How would she even know about it? Did you tell her, Turner?" Lord Grave demanded.

"Most certainly not. We did exactly as you asked. Gave her a little information each time."

"She's a clever girl. She'll work out how to use it anyway," Lord Grave said.

"But how could she have left the library?" Mr Turner asked.

At that very moment, Bathsheba began growling again. Then Lucy heard a snuffling noise.

Lucy quivered in her hiding place behind the curtains. Any second now, Bathsheba was going to sniff her out. Moving as quietly as she could, she took the scarf and the tin from her bag. She wound the scarf over her mouth and nose and loosened the lid of the tin before flinging the curtain aside.

"Lucy!" Lord Grave bellowed and stepped towards her.

"Dear girl," Mrs Crawley chimed in.

"Keep away from me, all of you!" Lucy lobbed the tin she was holding at Lord Grave. The loosened lid flew off and a bright orange cloud of Extra Violent Mustard Mix immediately engulfed Lucy's enemies. Lucy turned away to avoid any stray puffs of the mustard, but even so, her eyes began to water. With tears streaming down her face, she yanked the library window open and climbed outside. Behind her, she could hear Lord Grave and the others coughing, spluttering and sneezing. Good. They deserved to suffer.

Lucy crouched on the stone windowsill for a few seconds. She pulled the scarf down round her neck and breathed in the fresh, clean air while planning her next move. The ivy growing past the window was her only hope. Would it hold her? Maybe not with the added weight of the Wish Book. So she threw the bag containing the book on to the grass below, hoping that it wouldn't get damaged. Then she began climbing down the ivy.

But the ivy had other ideas.

Lucy was halfway down the ivy when it began to poke into her ears and nose and mouth and generally make a nuisance of itself. But she didn't panic. She'd suspected the ivy might be one of the measures Mr Turner had said were in place to protect the library and so she had come prepared. Blinking away tears (the ivy's exploration of her nostrils was making her eyes water again), Lucy hung on to the ivy with one hand and fumbled around in her pocket with the other, taking out the shears she'd stolen from Vonk. She began hacking away at the creeping plant, which hissed and wriggled like an angry snake and began to shrivel. It loosened its hold just long enough for her to climb further down and then leap the last few feet to the ground.

Sounds of coughing and sneezing and raised voices were still coming from above. Lucy looked up. A few drops of rain fell on her upturned face. No, not rain. A fine mist of water was drifting down from the library window. Lord Grave must have magicked up some sort of shower in the library to damp down the Extra Violent Mustard Mix. She had to get going before he, Bathsheba and Mrs Crawley recovered enough to pursue her. Lucy raced across the grass, the bag holding the Wish Book banging painfully against her hip. She sped round to the back of the house and into the kitchen where Becky and Smell were having a sly nap.

"What's going on?" Becky said, jerking awake. But Lucy didn't reply. She whizzed past and out again, up the stairs and off towards the Room of Curiosities.

CHAPTER SIXTEEN

HAVOC CREATED

"I've got it, I've got it!" Lucy shouted, when she'd hurriedly taken the glass cover off the raven.

"The Wish Book? You managed it?" the raven said, stretching out his metal wings in triumph. "Brilliant girl!"

"But he knows. Lord Grave knows I've stolen it. He'll work out where I am, any second!" Lucy's words came out in a frantic tumble.

"Open the book," the raven said, hopping to the ground.

Lucy sat on the cold marble floor and did as the raven said.

"But how does it work? Oh no! You can't tell me, can you?"

The raven stared at Lucy. "Drat it! That's right!"

"You can write it though, like last time?"

"Of course I can!" The raven darted over to a dusty corner of the room as before. Lucy followed him, carrying the Wish Book. Again using his beak as a pen, the raven wrote:

26 pages. Page 1=A

Lucy gazed at the raven and shook her head, not understanding.

"Think. Think about the pages. What else has twenty-six parts?" The raven said urgently.

Lucy put her hands to her head, willing her brain to think fast. "The alphabet. I see! The first page is A, the second B and so on like that!"

"Yes! What do the words on the first page say?"

"*To Wish, Spell.* So I have to . . . spell out the wish?"

"Yes! Yes!" The raven took flight and flew around the room, cawing wildly.

"What should I wish for exactly?" Lucy shouted up at him.

The raven landed and scuffed over the dust with his claws before writing in it again. This time he wrote:

CREATE HAVOC.

"*That's* what I have to wish for? Create Havoc? What will that do? Cause a distraction so we can escape?"

"In a manner of speaking."

"But what about wishing I was back with my mother and father? What about Violet and the others?"

"We can attend to all that afterwards. Think, Lucy, think. If you wish yourself back home with your parents, then that's where you'll be, not here. How then will I get free? How will we help the other children?"

"Can't you make your wish afterwards?"

"No. I'd still be raven-formed. The Wish Book only works with a human's touch. Please, Lucy. We need to hurry. If we don't . . . we may not be in time to save your little friend."

Lucy sat down again and opened the Wish Book. She ran her fingertips over the three holes that represented the letter C. After that, she turned to the eighteenth page, R, then continued back and forth over the pages, the cold metal growing warm under her fingers.

At last, she reached the final C of *CREATE HAVOC* and was about to run her fingers over the corresponding three holes when something needle-sharp plunged into her shoulder. It was Smell. He was clinging to her, digging his claws in.

"Arrgh! Where did you come from? Get off me!" she cried. "Get off!"

"The last letter! The last letter!" shrieked the raven, flapping its wings. It launched itself at Smell and grabbed the cat's tail in its beak, dragging him off. Lucy shrieked in pain as Smell's claws raked the back of her neck. The two animals fell to the floor in a snarling tangle of metal and fur.

Eyes watering in pain, Lucy used her sleeve to wipe

away the blood trickling down her neck. Then she brushed her fingers over the three holes that stood for C. In the same instant that her fingers touched the final hole, Smell and the raven stopped fighting.

"Cccccckkkkkk!" said the raven, before keeling over backwards. It lay motionless, legs pointing towards the ceiling.

Lucy dropped the Wish Book in shock.

"You killed him, you stupid, stupid animal!" she shouted at Smell.

Smell was backing away from the dead raven, growling, belly low against the ground, his one and a half ears flattened against his skull. Black smoke began billowing from the raven's chest, as though its heart was on fire. Before Lucy could fathom this, the smoke filled the Room of Curiosities, blinding her and making her throat burn and itch. She staggered about, coughing. The smoke grew even thicker and swirled around her. So did horrible thoughts.

I'm going to die here.

I'll never get home to Leafy Ridge. Never see Mother or Father again. Violet will meet a horrible end. And

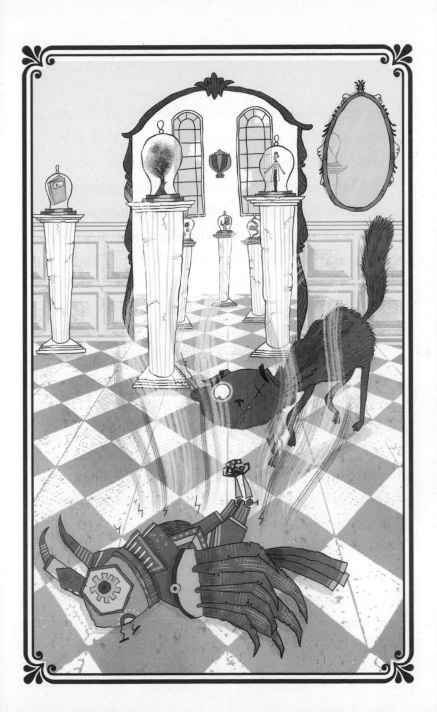

no one will ever discover what happened to all the other stolen children. Lord Grave and Ma'am and the others will have got away with it.

She shook her head to clear it. Thinking of her father had reminded her of something. Because he so often nearly set the kitchen alight when he was scorching pies, Lucy had taken the trouble to learn some basic fire safety. So she knew that she should keep as close to the ground as possible where the air was fresher. She dropped to the marble floor and began to crawl along. But the smoke quickly blackened and thickened even more. She heard Smell wail pitifully. The smoke gathered itself into a thin whirling tube, like a hurricane. Light flickered and crashed at the centre of the hurricane, growing brighter and brighter. The light swallowed the smoke and then flashed hard and fast and loud, dazzling Lucy and making her ears ring.

When the light faded and she could see again, the last of the smoke was drifting in dark wisps towards the ceiling.

In place of the whirling hurricane stood a tall thin man.

CHAPTER SEVENTEEN

A COMPLETE DISASTER

Smell leaped at the man's face, teeth bared, claws unsheathed. But the man was ready for him, grabbing the scruff of his neck before flinging him away. Smell crashed into some of the other curiosities in the room and lay motionless where he fell, amongst shards of glass.

As for Lucy, before she could do anything, the man reached down and whipped the scarf from round her neck, using it to tie her hands together behind her back. Then he forced her face down on the ground and used the trailing ends of the scarf to tie her ankles together before taking a handkerchief from his pocket and tying it round her mouth. Lucy hoped that the handkerchief was at least clean.

With Lucy safely trussed up, the man bent over the charred remains of the raven. What was left of the bird's metal casing was melting away, leaving a skeleton behind. Small black buds sprouted from the bones, blossoming into glossy black feathers. When it was fully restored, the raven struggled back to its feet, real feet now with real claws. It opened its beak and cawed before fluttering on to the man's shoulder.

"Nevermore, we are ourselves again. Free," said the man. His voice was that of the clockwork raven. He straightened the very old-fashioned three-cornered hat he wore and retied the blue ribbon fastened at the end of his long pigtail, which was black, threaded with grey.

The bird on his shoulder replied in a creaky, cackling voice, "Indeed, but we mustn't stay here. What are you planning to do with the girl?"

"Take her with us," the man replied.

"No!" Lucy shouted. "You can't! You said you'd get me back home! And what about Violet and the stolen children? We need to tell someone what's happening!" But of course her mouth was stuffed with handkerchief, so this just came out as, "Mmmph!"

"I think little Lucy is upset," said the man. Then he bent down, his dark brown eyes meeting hers.

"I lied, I'm afraid," he said.

"One of his many bad habits," Nevermore remarked from her perch on the man's shoulder.

The man straightened up and strode over to the Wish Book, which Lucy had left lying on the floor, but he didn't pick it up.

"Do it quickly! They'll be here soon!" shrieked Nevermore.

"Patience. I need the girl's help," the man said. Then he whispered something to Nevermore, who hopped off his shoulder, fluttered over to Lucy and landed on her head. Lucy screamed as the bird clawed at her scalp and began pulling out strands of hair with her beak. Tears of pain and rage trickled down Lucy's face.

"Excellent!" said the man.

"Enough?" said Nevermore.

"For now."

The man crouched next to Lucy again and dipped each of his fingers in the tears trickling down her cheeks. When each fingertip was wet, the man held them in front of his face. White sparks danced and sizzled over his hands.

"Now we can begin," said the man, picking up the Wish Book. He opened it and began turning the pages back and forth with the fingers he'd dipped in Lucy's tears. He worked so quickly, the pages blurred.

A second later, Lord Grave, Bathsheba, Vonk and Mrs Crawley all came crashing into the Room of Curiosities, tumbling over each other in their haste. When they'd scrambled to their feet (and paws), they stood gawping at Lucy, Nevermore (who was still perched on the back of Lucy's head) and the strange man.

"Havoc Reek. So you're free," Lord Grave said. Bathsheba stood next to him, growling.

"Credit where it's due, Grave. You've done well

to keep us this long. That was a clever enchantment, although a little cruel, don't you think?" Havoc Reek said, continuing to spell with the Wish Book.

"You took my son!" Lord Grave bellowed, although it was a hoarse sort of bellow due to the after-effects of the Extra Violent Mustard Mix.

Havoc Reek made a scoffing noise.

Lucy remembered the painting of Lady Grave and Little Lord Grave. Vonk had said that little Lord Grave was dead. Had this man killed him?

"Let the girl go," Lord Grave said.

"I could. But I won't. Come any nearer and Nevermore will peck a hole in her jugular. She'll die in seconds."

Nevermore hopped on to Lucy's shoulder blade and Lucy felt the cold sharp jab of the bird's beak against her neck. Smell, who had recovered by now and was crouched next to Lord Grave and Bathsheba, yowled and wriggled his bottom, as though preparing to pounce.

"You don't have any power to escape. The Wish Book won't work for you now," Lord Grave said.

"You'd be surprised." Havoc's fingers grew still. He looked up from the Wish Book. At the same time a slash appeared in mid-air, a ragged bright slash like the one Lucy had seen above the driveway when Lord Grave's dinner guests had arrived.

"Don't do it!" Lord Grave stepped forward menacingly. "We'll find you anyway."

"No nearer!" Havoc screamed and grabbed Lucy.

The slash opened wider. Became a hole. There was nothing but darkness inside it.

"Let her go. I won't stop you escaping if you do," Lord Grave said.

"I know why you want her. She comes with me. So does the Wish Book."

Lord Grave lunged at Havoc, but it was too late. Havoc pushed Lucy head-first through the hole, as though he was threading a giant needle. As Lucy felt herself fall, she heard a familiar gruff accented voice say, "Wet my whiskers, Grave, this is a complete disaster."

She briefly recognised it as the voice from the argument she'd overheard outside the drawing room, and wondered again who it belonged to.

Then the darkness took her.

Lucy shivered and opened her eyes. Her arms and legs were stiff and cold. It was as though she'd fallen asleep on one of the chilly marble slabs that kept Bathsheba's meat cold in Mrs Crawley's pantry. She was lying on her side in a round room with grey, curved stone walls and a high narrow window made of glass crisscrossed with strips of black metal. Snow was piled up against the outside of the window. Havoc suddenly loomed over her with Nevermore on his shoulder. He untied the handkerchief from her mouth.

"This isn't Leafy Ridge! This is somewhere else entirely! You tricked me!" Lucy blurted out.

"No. I saved you. Saved you from Grave. He'd have followed us in a trice if I'd taken you home. I'm on your side, remember?"

"You ripped half my hair out! How is that being on my side?"

"It was a very stressful situation. I may have acted

a little forcefully. Spoken immoderately. I'm going to untie you now. I trust you not to do anything stupid. You need to trust me in return. Do we have agreement?"

Lucy wasn't at all sure she could trust this man and his vicious companion. He *had* freed her from Lord Grave's clutches, but he'd also threatened to kill her. Still, she had little choice but to play along for the time being. "I suppose so."

"You're going to be friends? How touching," cawed Nevermore as Havoc began untying Lucy.

"I'll be back shortly," Havoc said when Lucy was finally free. He turned on his heel and left, with the Wish Book tucked under his arm and Nevermore on his shoulder. Lucy heard him locking the door behind him.

After what seemed like hours, Havoc and Nevermore finally returned. Havoc was bundled up in a cloak trimmed with fur. Lucy stared at it jealously. She'd been pacing around the room for ages trying to keep warm.

"Where are we and what exactly is happening? And what about Violet and the other children? What

are we going to do about them?" Lucy said.

"Have some patience, Lucy. It will all become clear. Let's get out of here, it's freezing." He pulled his cloak tighter round himself.

"I had noticed," Lucy said, blowing on her blue and frozen fingers.

"So insolent!" said Nevermore. "Shall I peck one of her eyes to quieten her down? Hazel ones are my very favourite. I particularly enjoy sucking out the middle part. So very tasty! Yum yum!" She flapped around Lucy's head, forcing her to follow Havoc out of the room and to the bottom of a stone staircase.

"Do try to be nice, Nevermore," Havoc said, grabbing Lucy's arm and pulling her up the narrow stone steps. They twisted and turned until Lucy grew so dizzy she was almost glad Havoc had such a strong hold of her. At last, the stairs ended. Ahead lay a passageway lined with arched windows.

Lucy wrenched her arm from Havoc's grasp and darted over to one of the windows, hoping to work out where she was. She glimpsed a flat frozen landscape that stretched for miles, white and empty.

Snow drifted from the night sky.

"Come on," Havoc said, dragging her away.

They reached a huge wooden door studded with black metal. Havoc turned the ring-shaped handle and opened the door. He strode over the threshold with Lucy firmly in tow.

At least this room was warm and bright. A friendly yellow glow came from several tall candelabras and a fire crackling in an enormous stone fireplace. A woman stood with her back to Havoc and Lucy, warming her hands over the flames. Her hair was red and she wore a warm-looking scarlet dress with black fur collar and cuffs.

The woman turned.

At once, Lucy twisted out of Havoc's grip and scrambled her way back to the door. She fumbled for the handle. But Havoc was on her in a second, forcing her into the room again. She had no choice but to face the woman who had given her nightmares all these years.

Lady Red.

CHAPTER EIGHTEEN

LADY RED

"Hello, sweet child. What a wonderful surprise. I could hardly believe it when Havoc told me you were here," said Lady Red.

"This is Amethyst Shade. Are you pleased to be reunited?" Havoc was behind Lucy, but she could hear the smugness in his voice. She tried to stamp her heel down on his toes, but missed.

Amethyst Shade smiled. The light from the fire

behind her cast a halo round her hair.

Afraid to meet Amethyst's eyes, the eyes that she'd seen so often in her nightmares, Lucy stared at the walls instead. Then wished she hadn't. The wallpaper depicted wild-eyed, long-fanged beasts eating smaller, more unfortunate creatures. Lucy shifted her gaze to the ceiling, where several small, blue glass bottles dangled from silver chains.

"Havoc, perhaps you might leave us now so Lucy and I can have a talk," Amethyst said.

"Of course." Havoc smiled a thin-lipped smile and bowed slightly. "We can get together later, my dear."

"Call me that again and I'll be forced to do something unspeakable to you." For a second, Amethyst's eyes glowed in the unnatural way they had in Lucy's nightmares. If only mentally slamming a door could save Lucy now. But there was no escaping this terrifying woman any longer.

"You mustn't mind Havoc," Amethyst said when the two of them were finally alone. Her voice was surprisingly warm and gentle and her eyes had returned to a more normal blue colour. "He can be somewhat . . . acerbic, but he means well. Although I must admit that bird is a complete ruffian. But listen to me, chattering on while you're nearly dead with exhaustion. Please. Sit down and rest."

Lucy's trembling legs were grateful for the offer and so she collapsed into one of the chairs next to the fire. Her head was spinning as she tried to make sense of everything.

"Don't be afraid, Lucy. You'll be safe here. I mean you no harm," Amethyst said.

"I haven't got the card," Lucy blurted out. "It's at Grave Hall. I'm sorry I stole it!"

"I don't care about the card," said Amethyst, smiling in a reassuring way. "It was never about the card. It was about you being safe. I knew he wanted to take you, even then."

"Who? Lord Grave?" Lucy said, feeling increasingly bemused.

"Oh, my poor child, you're shivering. I'm so sorry, you must be perished." Amethyst went over to a wardrobe in the corner of the room, took out a fur-lined cloak, and brought it to Lucy, who wrapped herself in it, grateful for its warmth. Then she took a chair and set it opposite Lucy.

"As I said, Grave had his eye on you, so I kept my eye on him. But then you stole the card from me. I tried to find you again, but I couldn't. Sometimes I felt I was getting close. I'm not sure if it was magic or instinct but I could sense you nearby. But then, almost like having a door slammed in my face, I'd lose you again. It was as though you had vanished."

"I didn't go anywhere."

"How strange. Now tell me, what do you know about Grave's activities? Has Havoc told you anything?"

"He couldn't tell me much because of his enchantment, the one Lord Grave put on him."

"What a clever . . . enchantment."

"But I do know some things. I overheard Lord Grave talking to a horrible, thuggish-sounding man who I think works for a woman they call Ma'am. Lord Grave and the others have been kidnapping children on her orders. But I don't know exactly why."

Amethyst's eyes grew brighter for a second and Lucy was afraid she'd made her angry. But then

Amethyst simply sighed sadly. "Yes, the mysterious Ma'am. Her identity has always been kept secret, but I'm doing my best to find out who she is. Oh, it's all so very evil, but so very clever. Taking children who won't be missed by anyone. Orphans. Neglected children whose parents don't care about them."

Lucy was about to say, *but I'm not an orphan. My parents don't neglect me.* But then she remembered how terrible life had been before she met Amethyst and stole the card. How her parents kept gambling, even when they didn't have enough to eat. So it wasn't surprising that she might have appeared somewhat uncared for.

"What do they do to the children they steal?" Lucy asked fearfully.

Amethyst left her seat and walked over to the window. She stared out at the snow for a few seconds. "Children are full of love, energy and curiosity. This makes them powerful in ways that are lost when they become adults. Grave, Ma'am and their cronies want to take that power for themselves. They use terrible magic to drain it out of children, not caring if they die in the process." Amethyst turned back to Lucy. Tears

were streaming down the woman's cheeks.

Lucy's own eyes blurred. "They have my friend Violet," she said in a small voice. "She's only little."

Amethyst came over to Lucy's chair and crouched beside her, taking Lucy's cold hands in hers. They felt warm and soft. "Don't despair. There's always hope. And at least you're safe now, here with me."

"Where is *here*, exactly?"

"It's best you don't know where you are, sweet child. What you don't know can't be . . . forced out of you."

"We're a long way from Grave Hall, though, aren't we? So why did it only take a few minutes to get from there to here?"

"That's because you came by magic. Using normal methods of transport would take weeks."

"Can Lord Grave use magic to get here too?" Lucy said, suddenly afraid that she wasn't really safe after all.

"No one can come within several miles of this tower without my say-so."

"If you're a magician too, why can't you do something to stop Lord Grave and Ma'am and the rest of them?"

Amethyst's face grew solemn. "We tried in the past. Havoc and I. But when Grave found out what we were up to there was a battle. We fought hard, but Grave and his minions are very powerful."

"And Ma'am too?"

"Yes. Ma'am was involved too, of course. We lost, and we found ourselves stripped of our magic and helpless. They caught Havoc and enchanted him, as you know. But I was luckier. I managed to retain just enough of my magic to escape and hide here."

"If you've been stripped of your magic, does that mean you're trapped here?" Lucy asked, anxious that she might be trapped too, if that was the case.

"It's complicated to explain. But I can still use magic temporarily to leave here and for long enough to thwart the kidnappers."

"What about the police? If you told them what was happening they could help, couldn't they?"

"I'm like you, Lucy. I'm from a poor family. No one would take my word against Grave's."

Lucy nodded slowly. She'd been in the same boat, so she understood. "So how have you been thwarting the kidnappers?"

Amethyst smiled and her eyes glowed again, not with anger this time, Lucy thought, but with triumph. "I'll show you."

Amethyst took Lucy's hand and led her out of the room and back down the twisty stone staircase to the floor below, then along a passageway with a door at the end of it.

"Now, I hope this will be a pleasant surprise for you." Amethyst put her hand on the doorknob, then stopped. "One thing, Lucy. Don't mention Ma'am to anyone just yet. I want to find out exactly who she is first. And I don't want any of my guests made more afraid than they already are or to have information that could put them in danger later on."

"Guests?"

"You'll see," Amethyst smiled warmly as she opened the door to a large round room. Like the room Lucy had just been in, it had a huge fireplace and tall candelabras. Thick, jewel-coloured rugs covered the floors. One was rolled up and a game of hopscotch was chalked out on the stone flags. A boy and a girl sat at a table with a game of chess laid out in front of them. They both looked up as Amethyst and Lucy entered.

"Hello, Mother! Have you rescued someone new? I didn't know you were going out!" said the boy. His wavy black hair was shoulder-length and he had thick black eyebrows.

"I'll explain later, Bertie. This is Lucy Goodly. The poor child has been incarcerated at Grave Hall until now. Can I leave her with you to settle in?"

Bertie sprang to his feet. "Of course!"

Amethyst gave Lucy a quick hug. "I'll see you very soon, sweet child," she said and left the room.

Lucy stood there, feeling rather awkward, until the boy laughed (he had a nice laugh, she thought) and said, "Don't look so worried, we don't bite! I'm Bertie. And this is Kathleen." He pointed at the girl he'd been playing chess with.

The door flew open and another girl came running in. She was smaller and younger than Kathleen and Bertie. When she saw Lucy she stopped. Stared.

And then burst into tears.

CHAPTER NINETEEN

NEW FRIENDS AND OLD FRIENDS

L ucy ran to Violet and hugged her. The little girl's
body shook with sobs.

"I was so afraid for you. I thought *he* would
have done something horrible to you by
now," Violet managed to choke out. "I felt so bad that
I was safe and you weren't."

"I think you both need to sit down," said Kathleen.
"Come on over by the fire."

Dazed with shock and relief at finding Violet in

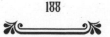

this strange place, Lucy allowed herself to be led over to one of the armchairs grouped round the fireplace. There was a kettle hissing on the hob. Kathleen bustled around making them all a cup of tea.

"How did you end up here, Violet? Everyone at Grave Hall has been looking for you." Lucy asked when she'd recovered a little, sipping the tea that Kathleen handed her.

"I bet they have," said Violet. She began to sob again.

"Don't cry, Violet, you're safe here, you know that." Kathleen perched on the edge of Violet's armchair and put her arm round the little girl.

Lucy suddenly remembered Caruthers. He was still in her pocket. "Look who I have with me. He's a bit messed up, but we can mend him," she said, handing the frog to Violet.

"Oh, Lucy! Thank you so much!" Violet hugged Caruthers tightly. "Look, Kathleen. This is my little Caruthers! Do you remember I told you how much I missed him?"

"Of course I do. I'm so glad you have him back.

Now Lucy, why don't you tell us what happened to you?"

So Lucy told Bertie, Kathleen and Violet everything, although she didn't mention Ma'am as Amethyst had instructed. They all listened intently. Although every now and then, when Lucy mentioned anything magic-related, Bertie made a tutting sound. Eventually, Lucy broke off her tale.

"What is it? Why are you doing that *tsk-tsk* thing? Do you think I'm lying?"

Kathleen said, "Bertie doesn't believe in magic."

"How can you not believe in magic? Amethyst's your mother. How can you have a magician for a mother and not believe in magic? Aren't you magical too?"

"If you mean, have I inherited Mother's special mental abilities, no, I haven't. But lots of what you're calling 'magic' can actually be explained scientifically. I have books about it. And the stuff we can't explain, well, that's just because we haven't made the right discoveries yet," Bertie said, fiddling nervously with a piece of cord he wore round his neck.

"We?" Lucy said.

"Scientists."

"You're a scientist?"

Bertie nodded.

Lucy raised her eyebrows at Kathleen, who shook her head slightly. So instead of arguing the point further, Lucy turned to the little scullery maid.

"Will you tell me what happened to you, Violet?"

"My parents made me work all the time. They didn't want to get a job themselves. Just to loaf around all day, eating treacle pudding. They hired me out as a scullery maid to whoever paid the most money without caring whether I'd be safe or not. And it turns out I wasn't safe at all."

"Oh, Violet!" Lucy wished she had known all this before. Perhaps she could have done something to help? But then again, Violet had seemed happy enough at Grave Hall. Could she have been under some kind of spell?

"It was only when you met Amethyst that you found out the truth about Lord Grave, wasn't it?" Kathleen said.

"I was so lucky. I met her in Grave Village when I was doing some shopping for Mrs Crawley."

"Amethyst was in Grave Village. Why?" Lucy asked.

"Keeping an eye on Grave's activities, of course," Bertie said.

"I dropped my bag, and everything fell out. Amethyst helped me pick it all up," Violet continued. "She was so kind, she's *always* so kind. We got talking. I told her about my horrid parents and about working at Grave Hall. Then she told me the danger I was in. So she brought me here."

"Violet," Lucy said anxiously, "did Lord Grave ever hurt you?"

"No. But Amethyst said it was only a matter of time. She said I was full of energy and curiosity and that was just what he needed to make himself more powerful." Violet's voice trembled.

"And what about Becky? Do you think he tried to take her power?"

"I don't know. But she was always so horrible to us, wasn't she? Perhaps that was because something at Grave Hall was making her unhappy and scared."

"That might be true, I suppose. What about you, Kathleen? How did you end up here?"

"My parents loved the gin shop more than they loved me." Kathleen looked down at her hands. "I don't really like to talk about it."

"I'm so sorry. But at least you're safe now. Are there more of you here? There was a boy called Eddie taken recently. Is he all right?"

"Yes, Eddie was with us, just for a little while," Bertie replied.

"And what about Claire Small? And Harold Jameson? Deborah Jones?" Lucy explained how she had found their belongings when she crashed into the painted cabinet.

To Lucy's dismay, Bertie shook his head. "I don't know any of them. I'm sorry. Amethyst can't rescue all of the children that Grave kidnaps. It's impossible."

"That's awful," Lucy said. "That we're all safe here and they . . ."

"I know," Kathleen agreed. "I know."

"So what will happen to me? To us?" asked Lucy.

"You said Eddie left. Did he go back home? When will I go home?"

Bertie shook his head. "You'll never be safe with your own parents. Mother finds new families for the children she rescues, with decent magicians that are sympathetic and can offer protection."

"But I don't want to go to a new family. I want my own parents!" Lucy cried.

"Could they guard you against Lord Grave?" Bertie asked quietly. "Are they good parents?"

"I . . . well . . . they try." But Lucy knew in her heart that her parents were useless in many ways. They'd have no chance of keeping her safe. "But if there are other magicians out there willing to help, why don't they do something to stop Lord Grave?"

"There's not enough of them brave enough to stand up to him, Mother says," Bertie replied.

Kathleen laid a hand on Lucy's arm. "Amethyst is a good person. This is all part of her plan to defeat Lord Grave and everyone who is on his side. You have to trust her. Your life depends on it."

Lucy swallowed hard. "I know. I thought at first

she wanted to hurt me, not help me. But I *do* trust her now. Bertie, you must be really proud of your mother, of what she's doing."

"I am. But you know, she isn't my real mother," Bertie said quietly. "I had terrible parents too. They cared more about making lots of money than they did about me. Grave was their friend. He told them he had found a good boarding school. That I could stay there and they wouldn't need to bother with me until I was grown up. Of course, really he was planning to experiment on me. He was taking me away in his coach when Mother realised what was happening and rescued me. I'm lucky to be alive. We're *all* lucky that Mother rescued us in time."

That evening they all had dinner with Amethyst, except for Violet, who went to bed early, as the day's surprises had worn her out. The food served at Amethyst's table was very strange. Pickled fish. Berries. And a dish of something pinkish and jelly-like.

"What is that?" Lucy asked.

"Seal blubber – it's delicious. And studies by Blenkinsopp and Pratt show it's really good for you," Bertie said, helping himself to a spoonful.

Lucy thought Blenkinsopp and Pratt might be mistaken. She found herself thinking almost wistfully of the sausage and custard pie that Mrs Crawley had presented for the servant's supper a couple of nights ago. The berries she was eating suddenly seemed to stick in her throat. She still found it hard to accept the housekeeper-cum-cook was involved in Lord Grave's dreadful crimes.

"Is something wrong with the dinner, Lucy, my sweet?" Amethyst asked.

"It's lovely. Really it is. Um . . . is there any magic in it?" Lucy asked, and explained about the Grave Hall everlasting soup and chicken-with-more-body-parts-than-might-be-reasonably-expected.

"No, there's no magic in this food. It's not one of my skills," Amethyst said. "I would imagine that the cook at Grave Hall is an Eker, though. They often are."

"A what?"

"An Eker. They can make a little of something go a long way. So they're very economical cooks."

Lucy remembered what Paige and Turner had told her about magicians; how most had one or two particular skills. "Oh, I see. Which skills do you have, Amethyst?"

"I had many, Lucy. Or at least I did before they were taken from me."

"Me too," said Havoc, hastily swallowing his seal blubber. "Used to have dozens and dozens."

Lucy ignored Havoc's boasting. "So that means you were extra powerful?" she said to Amethyst.

"I suppose you could say that," Amethyst agreed.

"Has Lord Grave got lots of skills or just one or two?"

"He has many, much to the misfortune of us all," Amethyst sighed and shook her head.

Before Lucy could decide which of the hundred questions teeming in her mind to ask next, Amethyst said, "I think we should all get some rest. Kathleen, will you help me make hot chocolate for everyone?"

"Of course," said Kathleen, smiling.

"Lucy can have her hot chocolate in bed. Havoc, escort Lucy to the girls' room. She's still finding her way around and she might get lost."

Lucy really didn't fancy spending any more quality time with Havoc. "I'll be fine, I remember where to go."

"I insist, sweet child," said Amethyst. Her smile was as lovely as usual, but Lucy thought there was an impatient note in her voice.

"Very well," said Havoc, pushing back his chair. "Goodnight, my dear," he said to Amethyst, taking her hand and kissing the back of it.

Amethyst snatched her hand away and wiped it with her napkin.

As they made their way along the passage to the girl's bedroom, Havoc said, "I've been meaning to ask you – why do you always wear boy's clothes?"

Nevermore, who was on Havoc's shoulder, cackled.

"I've been meaning to ask you – why do you suck up to Amethyst so much?" Lucy retorted.

Havoc puffed out his chest. "She's a wonderful woman and immensely talented. And she would never dress in such an unbecoming way."

Lucy snorted. "This coming from a man in a tatty tricorn hat and a straggly pigtail? So last century."

Havoc opened his mouth, no doubt to utter another insult. But then he paused before saying, "Look. We need to try to get along. Trust each other."

Lucy was about to reluctantly agree when she remembered something. "Lord Grave said you took his son. If I'm to trust you, I need to know what he meant by that."

"Lord Grave has invented accusations against me to cover himself. I have it on good authority that the boy died by Grave's own hand in some kind of botched magical experiment. Now go and get some sleep."

CHAPTER TWENTY

SPINNING A YARN

The next day, Kathleen helped Lucy find some warmer clothes to wear. When Lucy explained that she didn't like dresses, Kathleen picked her out a pair of woollen trousers, furry boots and a shirt that had belonged to Eddie Robinson.

Suitably attired, Lucy was able to join the others outdoors to play in the snow, where she saw the outside of her new home for the first time. The tower's walls were made of lumpy, crumbly black stone and the whole thing listed to the right. The snowdrifts surrounding the tower reached to the windowsills of the first floor where the dayroom was. The girls' bedroom was on the second floor while Amethyst and Bertie had quarters on the third floor. Havoc and Nevermore were apparently sleeping in the attic rooms.

"Did Amethyst build the tower herself?" she asked Bertie.

"No. There was once a whole castle here, but it was destroyed centuries ago. This tower is all that's left."

"Does it have a name?"

"We just call it 'the tower'. Now, look, I've got something for you!" There was a pile of wood leaning against a nearby tree. Bertie selected some of it, presenting Lucy with what looked like two planks and two sticks with sharpened ends.

"They're skis," he explained. "Very efficient way of getting around in a snowy environment. Hunters and warriors have used them since the Middle Ages you know. I'll show you how."

Bertie proved to be a very good teacher and Lucy soon learned to use the skis to skate along the snowy plains. She and the others also had great fun climbing out of the dayroom window and zipping down the slope created by the snowdrift piled up outside.

Lucy began to enjoy her new friends and surroundings, and her first couple of days at the tower soon flew past. Those days were short though, as sunset came very quickly and everyone had to be safely inside before dark.

"The wolves come out at night," Violet had told Lucy, her eyes wide. "Amethyst says the wolves would eat me up as soon as look at me."

The long evenings were pleasant too. Lucy would play hide-and-seek or hopscotch with Violet or simply chat with Kathleen. She also argued with Bertie on the matter of science versus magic. Then, just before they went to bed, all the children would visit Amethyst in her cosy sitting room and sit round the fire. They'd drink delicious hot chocolate while Amethyst told them fairy stories. She'd act them out extravagantly, transforming herself into the part of a cruel parent,

a fairy godmother or a wicked enchanter, making everyone shiver or laugh.

Lucy found that she slept surprisingly soundly at the tower, although sometimes she was a little fuzzy-headed in the morning. Bertie informed her that was because she wasn't used to the change in altitude yet. Whatever the reason, she felt completely safe for the first time in her life. She began to realise how terrible and neglectful her parents had been. With every day that passed, she grew less desperate to get back to them and more grateful to Amethyst, and more and more fond of her. In fact, she began to secretly hope that Amethyst might decide to adopt her and become her mother for good, just as she had with Bertie.

But on her third night in the tower, Lucy didn't sleep as well as usual for some reason. Her dreams were full of stolen children, begging for help. Their cries woke her. Even when she opened her eyes, the cries didn't stop. For a few seconds she continued to hear a thin wailing, which then petered out. Lucy slipped from her bed, thinking perhaps Violet or Kathleen was having a nightmare. But when she lit her candle to check, she found that Violet was fast asleep and Kathleen's bed was empty.

Lucy sat on the side of her bed and decided to wait and see if the wailing started up again. It didn't.

A few minutes later, Kathleen came into the bedroom. She looked dazed and her eyes were very red.

"Are you all right?" Lucy asked.

"Of course," said Kathleen, getting into bed. "Why?"

"I wondered where you were."

"I was with Amethyst. She says everything's almost ready for me at my foster parents'. I'll be leaving soon." Kathleen yawned hugely and was asleep as soon as her head touched her pillow.

Lucy was about to go back to sleep too, when she heard voices in the corridor outside. Kathleen had left the door open slightly. Lucy tiptoed out of bed to have a closer listen.

". . . planting all that rubbish. Very impressive.

I can't wait to see the end result," Lucy heard a screechy voice say. It was Nevermore.

"I imagine you'll get your chance soon," Havoc replied.

"Won't the other dear children wonder?"

"Oh, Amethyst spins a good yarn. She always has a convincing explanation ready."

The voices faded as Havoc and Nevermore went upstairs.

Lucy's feet were freezing from standing on the cold stone floor. She hurried back to bed, thinking about what she had just heard.

Amethyst spins a good yarn. Did that mean Amethyst was lying about something and if so, what? And why?

The next morning, Lucy was greeted by an excited Violet bouncing on her bed.

"Come on, let's go outside!"

Lucy unglued her eyes.

"Please hurry – we have to build a snowman before the sun goes away again!"

Lucy sat up in bed and blinked wearily. She felt as

though she'd only fallen asleep a few minutes ago.

At that moment, Kathleen came into the bedroom. She seemed to notice Lucy wasn't quite feeling up to par and said, "Violet, come on, let's go down to the dayroom. Bertie's there. We can have a game of hopscotch while Lucy's getting ready."

Feeling relieved to be alone for a few minutes, Lucy poured a bowlful of icy water from the jug that sat on the chest of drawers next to her bed. After a chilly wash that made her break out into goose bumps, she quickly dressed herself. Despite the lack of sleep, her mind felt sharper than it had for days.

Amethyst spins a good yarn.

Although she kept telling herself it meant nothing, that Amethyst had no reason to lie about anything, she couldn't help feeling a prickle of unease.

Lucy looked around the room. It was warm and comfortable, and she still felt grateful to be here, to be safe, to be alive, not like poor Claire Small and the others. But somehow the room was stifling too. Like wearing a shirt with a too tight-collar that made it difficult to breathe properly.

And so, when Lucy finally left the bedroom and found herself alone in the corridor, she made a sudden decision. It was time to do some exploring, some sneaking around. She should have done this before, instead of accepting everything she'd been told. It was most unlike her usual curious self.

Lucy crept up the spiral stone staircase to the third floor, where Amethyst and Bertie's rooms were. But just as she reached the top of the steps, there was a rustling behind her.

"Lucy! Good morning, sweet child. I hope you slept well. Did you want me for something?"

"We're going outside. I said I'd meet the others in the dayroom."

"The dayroom's downstairs," said Amethyst.

"Oh, I thought it was upstairs. I must have got muddled," Lucy said, trying to sound cheerful and not at all worried.

Amethyst said nothing.

"I'll be off and join the others now," Lucy continued, trying to sound unconcerned.

"It's very strange you should be so . . . muddled.

You've been here three days now. I would have thought you'd know your way around. Is everything all right?" Amethyst said.

"Yes. I'm just tired. I didn't sleep very well."

"Hmm, I see. Well, have fun in the snow. Remember now, back before dark. Night can be dangerous here, as you know."

Heart thumping, Lucy hurried down to the dayroom. The feeling of safety she had experienced over the last few days was beginning to fade. She wasn't quite sure why. At least not yet. But she was determined to find out.

CHAPTER TWENTY-ONE

THE TEAR CATCHER

"Bertie, isn't it boring for you, stuck here all the time?" Lucy asked as they were rolling a snowball big enough for a snowman's body, while Violet was making the head. Kathleen wasn't with them. She had decided to stay inside and read by the fire.

"It can be. But now I'm older Mother takes me with her sometimes when she visits the outside world. I go to bookshops, museums and libraries. That's how

I discovered science. And of course, since Mother started rescuing children I have some company."

Lucy fiddled with the hood of her cloak. "It's very dangerous for Amethyst, isn't it? What if Lord Grave catches her?"

"She doesn't seem to worry about that. She's so brave. You know she tried to keep exactly what she was doing a secret from me at first, because she didn't want me to be worried? I've only known for a few months."

Lucy frowned. "But I thought you said you were one of the first children Lord Grave targeted and Amethyst rescued you?"

"Yes, that's right. But I thought I was a one-off, the only child she'd rescued. I had no idea what she was doing."

"So how did you find out?"

"She came back late one night with one of the children. She thought I was asleep, but it was a clear night and I'd stayed up and sneaked out on to the tower roof. I'm very keen on astronomy, you see. So I saw she had a boy with her when she came back. And then she explained what she was doing. Since then I've helped her look after the children she rescues."

"I still don't quite understand how Amethyst can leave here to do the rescuing? Doesn't that mean she has to use magic? I thought she'd lost her magic when she fought with Lord Grave and the others?" Although Lucy remembered that Amethyst had mentioned she could use magic temporarily, she had never explained how this was possible.

"Her special mental abilities, you mean?"

"Can't we just call it magic? It makes it less confusing?"

"But it's not accurate!"

"Oh, never mind. Just tell me!"

"Well, Mother says she hid some of her abilities here in the Tower a long time ago because she was worried Grave might get her. She can absorb enough of them to leave for a few hours and do what she needs to. But she can't stay away for longer than that because all her abilities would weaken and she wouldn't be able to come back."

"So the Tower sort of tops her magic up? Like

refilling a jug?"

"Something like that."

"I see. Bertie, when I saw Amethyst for the very first time, she didn't seem like she was on a rescue mission. She was playing poker."

Bertie shrugged. "She gambles now and again. She says we need the money."

Lucy was silent for a while, weighing up what Bertie had told her. It all *sort of* made sense still. But what about the wails she'd heard last night and Kathleen's odd behaviour? And what about the strange conversation she'd overheard between Havoc and Nevermore? A bad feeling began to grow inside Lucy, but she tried to ignore it for now and concentrated instead on rolling the snowman's body. When it was finished, she and Bertie helped Violet attach the head.

"It needs a face," Violet declared when the snowman was complete.

Bertie handed Violet three lumps of coal he'd brought for the snowman's eyes and nose.

"But he has to have a mouth too!" Violet pointed out.

"We can find something for his mouth tonight and bring it to him tomorrow," Bertie replied. "We need to get home now. It'll be dark soon."

✳

"You're very quiet tonight, Lucy, are you still tired?" Amethyst said that evening when they were all sitting round the fire in her sitting room, drinking their bedtime hot chocolate.

Lucy nodded, glad for a way to explain her worried silence.

"Drink up your chocolate – that'll help."

Lucy took a small sip. It *was* very soothing. She took another sip. It tasted rich and delicious. Her worries and suspicions began to fade. The cries she'd heard . . . well, she could have been half-asleep and imagined them. As for the conversation between Havoc and Nevermore, maybe she'd misheard what they'd said? Or misunderstood. It could all be perfectly innocent. When Havoc had said *Amethyst spins a good yarn,* he could have been talking about Amethyst's wonderful bedtime stories. Lucy decided she really was worrying about nothing. Amethyst was a wonderful, brave person who could be completely trusted.

She was about to take another mouthful of her hot chocolate when Bertie snatched it from her, gulping down the whole lot in one go. He handed the empty cup back to her, smiling cheekily. Lucy was about to tell him off, especially as he'd done the same thing the night before. But Amethyst got there first.

"Bertie!" Amethyst shouted. "What are you doing? How dare you?"

"It doesn't matter," Lucy said quickly, shocked at the way Amethyst had spoken to Bertie, whom she clearly adored.

"Of course it does!" Amethyst's eyes were glowing with rage.

Bertie looked aghast. "I'm-I'm sorry. I didn't mean to—"

"He only took a tiny drop. I'd drunk most of it."

This seemed to calm Amethyst down.

"Well, that's good. Bertie, don't let me catch you doing that again. It's most ungallant. Now, off to bed, everyone, except for you, Kathleen. I have some more exciting news to share about your new family!"

An hour after turning in, Lucy was still lying awake. Violet was sleeping soundly in the bed opposite. The Tower was peaceful. All Lucy could hear was the crackle and snap of the logs burning in the fireplace. Pulling the fur coverlet up under her chin she willed herself to stay awake and wait for Kathleen to return from her chat with Amethyst. But time dragged on and there was no sign of Kathleen. Lucy began to drift off . . .

"No, noooo!"

Lucy snapped fully awake and leaped out of bed, her heart racing. She definitely was not imagining that.

Someone began crying.

The crying grew louder, turned to wails.

Lucy ran over to Violet's bed, expecting the wailing to wake the little girl any second. But Violet was still fast asleep. Lucy shook her gently, then not so gently.

Violet slept on.

The wailing continued. A girl, Lucy was sure of it.

Not a woman, a girl.

Kathleen. It had to be.

Even though the wails filled Lucy with fear, she knew she had to find out what was happening. So she pulled on her clothes, lit a candle, then crept out of the bedroom and began tiptoeing down the twisting stone staircase, following the sounds. The closer she got to the bottom, the better she could hear the terrible heart-wrenching sobs. They made her want to run back to the safety of her bed and forget about finding out more. But she made herself carry on. She stole down the remaining steps and along the corridor.

A large black rat scurried across Lucy's path, the only animal apart from Nevermore that Lucy had ever seen in the Tower. It stopped in front of her, raised itself on its hind legs and sniffed the air, whiskers twitching, head turning from side to side.

But Lucy wasn't afraid. It was just a rat and she'd once shared a room with a family of them. She shooed this one away and it scuttled off.

She blew out her candle, fearful that she might be seen. Ahead of her, the door to one of the supposedly unused dungeons was open. The light spilling through the doorway was enough for her to see by.

The sound of Amethyst's voice joined the sound of sobbing.

"So your parents used to pawn your clothes to pay for their gin?" she sneered.

"I had to wear a sack for a dress and tie rags over my feet. It was terrible. Everyone stared and pointed and laughed." Kathleen began to cry again.

"There there, that's right, let it all out, sweet child," Amethyst said in a comforting way that suddenly sounded horribly false to Lucy's ears.

Lucy wiped her eyes, which were welling up in sympathy with Kathleen. The urge to run back to bed was stronger than ever now. But Kathleen had been so kind to her. And she'd looked after Violet too. Now it was time to repay that kindness. She had to find out what was happening and if she could do something to help her new friend.

She inched towards the half-open dungeon door and peered round the edge.

Kathleen was tied to a chair inside the dungeon.

Amethyst was bent over her, holding a blue glass bottle to the girl's face. It had a squat bulbous body with a long thin neck. At the top of the neck was a curved spout, which Amethyst was pressing underneath Kathleen's eye.

The bottle was catching Kathleen's tears.

"It's deeply interesting how she doesn't remember this has happened before," said Havoc, who was lounging against the dungeon wall, arms folded, Nevermore on his shoulder as usual.

"If she remembers anything she'll think we spent an hour book learning and discussing how lovely her new family is and how they're going to absolutely adore her," Amethyst said in a horrible mocking way.

"I do wish you'd let me have a try."

"Maybe next time."

"My dear, anyone would think you didn't want me to master the technique," Havoc said. He sounded suspicious.

"Havoc. What a ridiculous notion. Being enchanted for so long seems to have made you mistrustful. By all means, try it yourself." Amethyst held the blue bottle up to the light of the candelabra that stood in a corner of the dungeon. "A quarter full. I suppose it won't do any harm to let you fill it a little more tonight." She handed the bottle to Havoc. "Do not overdo it. I've lost a couple that way. It's a terrible waste."

Havoc took the bottle and Amethyst's place. He bent over Kathleen.

"Let me do the words!" cawed Nevermore.

Amethyst shook her head. "Havoc, I don't think—"

But the taunts were already tumbling from Nevermore's beak. "Ugly little guttersnipe. Shall I peck your nose away? Oh, perhaps not, it's far too fat and snotty. Urgh."

Kathleen pressed herself against the back of her chair. Although she no longer sobbed, tears kept streaming down her face.

"You think that little Bertie fancies you, don't you? How could he? You're far too revolting. He said as much to the new girl. She almost wet her drawers laughing at you. Everyone hates you really."

Kathleen's tears fell faster and faster.

Amethyst clapped her hands in delight, her eyes glistening in the candlelight. "Nevermore, you are a genius! I must plant that as a memory in her mind for next time. Now Havoc, the tears, quickly. These will be extra powerful, I think."

Havoc pressed the tear catcher to Kathleen's eye once more. It filled up to around halfway before Kathleen's sobs began to slow.

"Now give it to me." Amethyst stretched out her arm, clicked her fingers impatiently. Havoc fiddled with the chain that hung round the neck of the bottle. A silver stopper dangled from the end of it. He began pushing the stopper into the neck of the bottle.

"No! You don't stopper the bottle until—" Amethyst shouted.

Too late.

As Havoc clumsily jammed the stopper into the glass bottle, Kathleen . . . vanished. All that was left behind was the rope that had bound her to the chair and a puddle of her tears on the floor.

CHAPTER TWENTY-TWO

THE TRUTH ABOUT BERTIE

The floor seemed to tilt under Lucy. She grabbed the handle of the dungeon door to steady herself.

"Ah," said Havoc, staring at the puddle of tears.

"Ah?" screamed Amethyst. "Ah? She was one of the best I've ever found. A full bottle of her tears would have been immensely powerful."

"Well, perhaps you should have explained the process properly."

"I thought I had," Amethyst snapped.

She snatched the bottle of Kathleen's tears from Havoc, shook it, stared at it, then slipped it into a small bag tied at her waist. "I suppose it can go with the others. Every little helps."

"Do we have enough yet?"

"No. We need more, I keep telling you that. Each bottle only provides a certain amount of power for a limited amount of time. And some bottles are more powerful than others."

"How long do we have to wait before the latest one's ready? I want my revenge against Grave and the rest of them, Amethyst. *Magicians Against the Abuse of Magic* indeed. They were happy to abuse magic when they tried to destroy us. I can't wait to do the same to them."

Amethyst sighed. "Patience. It's proving difficult to plant new memories in her, even when she's asleep. Very unusual. With most children it's a matter of hours."

"What about the boy? Might give us something to be going on with."

"No. Never. No one touches Bertie. He's my son."

"Well, I suppose in a manner of speaking. But surely—"

Amethyst slammed Havoc against the stone wall, her hand round his neck. The whole dungeon shook as though there had been an explosion.

"He's my son. No one touches him. You'd better remember that," she yelled.

As Havoc gave a spluttered apology, Lucy took the opportunity to head for safety before she was seen and fled back to the girls' room. The first thing she did when she got there was to check Violet was still there. Relief washed over her when she saw the little girl was safely sleeping, with Caruthers on her pillow as usual. Lucy sat on the edge of Violet's bed, head in her hands, trying to think calmly and make sense of everything.

Havoc had mentioned something about *magicians against the abuse of magic*.

Magicians Against the Abuse of Magic.

MAAM.

Could it be that Ma'am wasn't a person, but some sort of organisation? A *good* organisation that Lord

Grave and the others were part of?

What was it Prudence Beguildy had said the night of the dinner party?

"... *Ma'am should act now that we have Eddie Robinson...*"

Lucy had thought this meant Lord Grave and his minions had Eddie and a person called Ma'am was going to do something terrible to him. But could Prudence have really been saying that MAAM needed to act now that Eddie had been kidnapped?

Then there was the handkerchief she'd found in Lady Sibyl's coach. The boxes of belongings in the cabinet. Perhaps they had all been things found at the scenes of various kidnappings? Perhaps Lord Grave and MAAM had been collecting clues too, hoping to solve the mystery of the missing children, not taking the children themselves.

And suddenly Lucy remembered that Eddie Robinson's parents had given an interview to the *Penny Dreadful*, saying how much they missed him. Why would they have done that if they didn't care about him?

As Lucy was working all this out, Violet cried out in her sleep, as though she was having a bad dream. Lucy was about to comfort her, but the little girl settled down again, pulling Caruthers closer.

Caruthers.

Violet's mother had embroidered Violet's name on him so he wouldn't get lost. Because she knew how much he meant to her daughter. That was the act of a kind, loving parent, not the horrible type Violet described. Why would she have lied?

'It's proving difficult to plant new memories . . .' Amethyst had said just now. Did this mean she was making the children she kidnapped believe their parents were awful and uncaring, so that they wouldn't want to go home? And then using the horrible false memories to make them cry and collect their tears. But why?

What was it Amethyst had told her that very first day? Something about children being powerful in ways adults weren't. That Lord Grave wanted to take that power. That he used terrible magic to drain children of it.

She was right – all that *was* really happening. Except it wasn't Lord Grave doing such dreadful deeds . . . it was Amethyst herself.

Amethyst spins a good yarn.

Lucy had been completely ensnared by those yarns and had got everything so, so wrong. She'd jumped to conclusions, making everything she heard and found fit with what she already believed was happening because she'd hated Lord Grave and wanted to believe the worst of him. She still didn't know why he had taken her away from her parents, but she now suspected that he might have had a very good reason for doing it. Why hadn't he told her those reasons? Probably because he knew how pig-headed, rude and downright stupid she could be!

But at least now she'd learned the truth. It was time to make a plan to get herself and Violet out of here. Some fast thinking was in order. She looked over at Violet, who was still fast asleep. How could she wake her, tell her such a terrible tale? She was so young.

And what about Bertie? Was he an innocent

victim too? Or was he yet another person who had lied to her? Although she'd only known him for a few days, she'd hoped they would become friends. But if he knew the terrible things Amethyst and Havoc were doing, he was no friend. He was her enemy. She had to take the chance to find out which he was. If she'd bothered to do that back at Grave Hall, bothered to tell Mrs Crawley or Vonk her fears, she probably wouldn't have made such a mess of things.

She opened the bedroom door and listened carefully.

Silence.

Amethyst and Havoc must have left the dungeon, Lucy thought. Hopefully they were safely asleep after their night's sinister exertions. Even so, Lucy's eyes and ears were on high alert as she made her way up to Bertie's room. Before she knocked on the door, she took a moment to marshal her thoughts. Caution was needed. She couldn't simply blurt everything out until she was certain how much Bertie already knew, if anything.

Finally, she took a deep breath and knocked at

the door. A few moments later, Bertie opened it. He was dressed in a long white nightshirt, his hair and eyebrows sticking up in a variety of directions. For a moment, his dishevelled state reminded her of someone, but she couldn't think who.

"Lucy?" He squinted at her. "What's wrong?"

"I need to talk to you."

"It's practically the middle of the night!"

"Shh! Please."

"Come in then."

Bertie's bedroom was spectacularly untidy. He didn't appear to understand the correct use of a wardrobe, as the huge wooden one that covered half a wall was standing with its doors open and nothing inside except for some books piled at the bottom. His clothes covered the floor.

Bertie looked down at his bare feet. "I'm going to get dressed first. Can't talk to you like this." He picked up a tangled bundle of clothes and went through a door in the far side of the room.

Lucy gazed around the chaotic room. There was a tall candelabra, taller than Lucy herself, standing next to a small desk. Hanging from it was the cord she had noticed Bertie wearing round his neck the day she arrived. A green velvet pouch dangled from it.

Look inside, a voice in her head suddenly urged. She untangled the cord from the candelabra. Weighed the pouch in her palm. It was heavier than she expected. She untied the knot in the drawstring and fumbled the soft velvet open.

Inside the pouch was a wooden ring with a small silver charm in the shape of a swan dangling from it. It took Lucy a few seconds to remember where she'd seen it before. And to remember again what Lord Grave had said to Havoc.

"*You took my son!*"

At that moment, Bertie burst back into the room. "What are you doing with that!" he shouted, snatching the ring out of Lucy's hand.

"Ssh, Bertie. Please. I can explain." Lucy sprang over to the bedroom door, which was half-open, and pushed it shut. "She mustn't hear."

"Who mustn't?"

"Amethyst."

Bertie scowled as he put the teething ring back in its pouch and draped the cord back round his neck. "Why? To think I was so excited when you arrived. I thought we'd be friends."

"We can be! You have to let me explain!"

"Friends don't snoop around each other's private stuff!" Bertie's voice was rising again.

"Please, Bertie. Stop shouting. I have to tell you something really, really important!"

"Ten seconds. That's it. Then I'm going to Mother. I'll tell her that you're nothing more than a nasty little thief. She can let Grave have you." Bertie glared at her with such disgust that Lucy began to feel quite sick.

"Your parents, Bertie. It's true that they were rich. But they didn't love money more than you."

Bertie's eyes widened. "What do you mean? How could you know that?"

Lucy pointed at Bertie's neck. "That teething ring. Where did you get it?"

Bertie touched the velvet pouch with his fingertips.

"Is that what it is? I found it in Mother's room." His face went very red.

Lucy went limp with relief. If Bertie had stolen the teething ring himself, he wasn't likely to go shouting to Amethyst about it. "Why did you take it, Bertie?" she asked gently.

"I found it a few months ago. She sent me to fetch something from her room. One of her cupboards was open and I found it. I can't explain why, but I . . . I had to take it. Then I was afraid that she'd realise what I'd done and be angry with me. So I thought if I wore it all the time, under my shirt, she'd never find out I had it. That doesn't make sense, I know. But the other thing is, it made me feel . . . good wearing it. Except . . ."

"Go on."

"If I wear it at night, I have these dreams. There's a woman. She's lovely. Kind. But the dreams make me feel so sad when I wake up. So a lot of the time I leave it off when I sleep."

"Bertie," said Lucy. "The woman's hair. Is it black but with a white streak, right at the front?"

Bertie went pale, fumbled his way to his rumpled bed and sat down. "How could you possibly know what I see in my dreams?" he whispered.

"I've seen her portrait in Lord Grave's house. She was his wife."

"Was? Does that mean..."

Lucy didn't want to say it, but she had to. "She's dead, yes. I'm so sorry. "

"Sorry? Why?"

"Bertie, the thing is – you're in the portrait too. I'm certain it's you as a baby. You're holding that same teething ring. The woman in your dream is Lady Grave, your mother. And Lord Grave is your father."

CHAPTER TWENTY-THREE

UNRAVELLING THE YARDS

"That's not true! Why would Amethyst lie to me?" Bertie wiped his face on his bed sheets.

"I really think it is true, Bertie – how would Amethyst have the teething ring if she hadn't taken you? And why would it make you think of Lady Grave if she wasn't your mother?

Bertie sat thinking for a long time, then looked up. "Well, if it is true I think I understand why Mother didn't want to tell me that I'm Lord Grave's son. The son of someone evil. That would be just like her to be so protective. Maybe Grave killed my mother and Amethyst took me – in case he killed me too?"

"No. I don't think so. Amethyst's been lying. I heard her say something about planting memories. I think she can make people remember things that never happened." She explained about Violet and Caruthers, and about Eddie Robinson's parents giving an interview to the *Penny*. "Parents who didn't care about their children wouldn't do any of that."

"That's true," Bertie said thoughtfully. "You know, I've read that people's minds can be manipulated. People have done experiments on it. But Mother wouldn't do that, I'm sure of it. Let's go and see her. Ask her. I'm sure she can explain everything."

"No, it's too dangerous!" Lucy found that her voice had suddenly turned wobbly. "I haven't told you why I came to see you yet. It's Kathleen. Something terrible has happened to her."

Lucy hated telling Bertie what she'd seen and heard. His face went from pale to green when she told him how Kathleen's tears were bottled and how Kathleen herself had vanished.

"I've seen those bottles in Amethyst's study. I asked her what they were. She said she was making a cordial. I tried to open one once, but I couldn't get the cork out. Imagine if I'd drunk it." Bertie shuddered.

"So you believe me?" Lucy almost wilted with relief.

Bertie nodded slowly. "It's all terribly unscientific, of course, but there is evidence to support what you've said. And why would you make all this up? There's no logical reason for you to lie as far as I can see." Bertie fell silent for a while.

Lucy broke that silence. "We have to leave here, take Violet. Get back to the outside world. You know how to do that?"

Bertie looked at Lucy; a look that told her he was gathering his courage for what lay ahead. "No, no, I don't."

"But you said Amethyst takes you there sometimes? You must have seen what she does to leave here?"

"I'm never awake for the journey. She puts me to sleep here and I wake up there. What about Havoc Reek?"

"Ask Havoc? Are you mad?"

"I don't mean that. He brought you here, didn't he? How did he do that?"

"He used the Wish Book. If only we knew where it is!"

"The what? Oh, is that the so-called magical book you told us about?"

"It's not so-called. It is!" Lucy said, hanging on to her temper by a thread.

"I've seen it! It's in her study."

"Why didn't you just say that? Come on!"

They ran out of Bertie's room and along the passageway to Amethyst's study. Once inside, they closed the door as quietly as possible and lit the candelabra.

A tall wooden cabinet stood against one wall of the study. There were drawers at the bottom, and the top half was made up of three shelves of books, which lay behind glass doors. Bertie took one of the books out of the cabinet and opened it. The pages inside had a hole cut in them and in that hole was a small key.

"You must have done a lot of poking around in Amethyst's things to find that out," Lucy whispered.

"Don't say it like that," Bertie whispered back, going red again. "There were times when there were just the two of us and then she'd go off for hours. There was nothing else to do except explore. But it's come in handy, hasn't it?"

Lucy had to admit it had.

Bertie took the key and opened one of the drawers. There was the bag Lucy had borrowed off Becky with the Wish Book inside it. Lucy lifted it out and explained to Bertie as quickly as she could how it worked.

"So you just spell out what you want to happen?" Bertie said. "But where are you going to wish us to?"

"Grave Hall. But as soon as I begin spelling out the wish, Amethyst will know what we're up to, I'm certain. There'll be trouble if she manages to follow us. We'll need help. Magical help."

"I think we should do the wish outside then.

If Mothe— I mean, Amethyst does realise what's happening, it'll take her that bit longer to get to us. She hates going out in the snow anyway. Ruins her shoes, she says."

Bertie's face was still very pale. How horrible all this must be for him. Amethyst had been a mother to him for five years. Now he'd discovered it was all a lie, that she'd stolen him from his loving father, and his real mother was dead.

"I'm sorry, Bertie. About everything."

"Don't you be sorry. Amethyst's the one to blame. And I'll pay her back for it one day," Bertie said, looking suddenly much older than twelve.

"We need to go. Let's get Violet. But there's one more thing we need to do. We can't leave these behind." She pointed up at the blue bottles dangling from the ceiling of Amethyst's study.

"Why do we need to take them?"

"Don't you see? One bottle of tears equals one child. Amethyst makes them cry themselves to death. And then she plans to take the power the tears hold for herself."

"And do what with it?"

"Get her revenge?"

"Does she *drink* them?" Bertie screwed up his face in disgust.

"I don't know. I don't really want to think about it."

"And Kathleen? Where is she? Do you think she's dead?"

"Her tears might be in one of these bottles, that's all I know."

"Can we find a way to get her back?"

"I don't know that either. But I am sure as I can be that if we take the bottles, we're taking away Amethyst's chance to get her full powers back and escape here for good. Come on, help me get them all down."

CHAPTER TWENTY-FOUR

THE SNOWMAN'S SMILE

"Why are we going out now? It's not even properly daytime yet. Where's Kathleen?" Violet said, blinking sleepily as Lucy helped her into furs and snow boots.

"It's a surprise. A special game. But you must keep very quiet. We'll see Kathleen soon."

Lucy turned away so that Violet wouldn't see the tears in her eyes. There'd be time to grieve for

Kathleen later. Right now, she needed to focus on getting everyone safely away. She touched the bag of bottles she and Bertie had taken from Amethyst's study.

"I'll get help for you as soon as I can, Kathleen. Maybe Lord Grave can bring you back," she whispered.

Bertie joined them, now bundled up in warm clothes.

"How are we going to get out?" he whispered to Lucy so that Violet wouldn't hear. "Amethyst locks the Tower doors at night."

"I've thought of that. We can ski out of the dayroom window, the same as the other day."

"Brilliant idea!"

They quickly gathered their skiing equipment together and went down to the dayroom. Bertie and Lucy hurriedly put their gear on and then helped Violet with hers. Bertie left first, skiing smoothly out of the dayroom window and down the snowdrift.

"You next," Lucy said to Violet.

"But what about the wolves?"

"Look." Lucy pointed at the sky. "It's nearly dawn. All the wolves will have gone now." She hoped this was true.

"All right then."

Lucy watched anxiously as Violet began the descent, but the little scullery maid kept her balance, although she crashed into Bertie at the bottom of the snowdrift, almost knocking him over. Then it was Lucy's turn. She was a little unsteady on her skis, and she was worried about falling and damaging the bottles and the Wish Book she was carrying in her bag. But she made it safely down to the others, her skis spraying snow as she came to a clumsy stop.

"Can we do it again?" asked Violet, her eyes shining and her cheeks glowing.

"Not right now," said Lucy. "Come on. I'll show you the surprise. I'll race you!" She wanted to get them further away from the Tower before using the Wish Book.

If she hadn't been escaping two twisted magicians who wanted to make her cry to death while bottling her tears, Lucy might have enjoyed skiing over the snow under a sky that was lightening into strips of pink and purple, the freezing air nipping her cheeks. But this was no game. They had to get as far away as fast as they could. Lucy risked a glance back at the Tower and her blood froze. There was no time to stop and check, but she thought she'd seen a face peering out of the dayroom window.

"Look, Lucy," Violet called after they'd gone a little way. "There's our snowman from yesterday! Can we build some more?"

"Not right now," Lucy said. "We need to go further."

"Wait! Stop!" Bertie shouted. He was just behind Lucy and Violet. They stopped dead and Bertie cannoned into them, nearly knocking them over.

"What's wrong?" Lucy asked.

"The snowman. There's something not right about it."

Lucy peered at the snowman. It looked just as it had yesterday, with its coal for eyes and nose.

"Look at its mouth," Bertie whispered.

A groove etched under the snowman's black nose gave its face an eerie smiling mouth.

"But we didn't give it a mouth," Lucy said.

"Exactly."

Lucy scrunched up her eyes. There was something glinting inside the snowman's smile. Something long and sharp.

"I want to play with it again!" Violet said, and before either Lucy or Bertie could stop her, she'd skied towards the snowman.

"Violet, come back!" Bertie shouted.

Suddenly the snowman roared and bared its icicle teeth. Teeth that none of the children had made when they'd built it. It bounced forward, then clamped its mouth round Violet's arm. Violet screamed, wide-eyed with shock and fear.

Lucy yelled and propelled herself towards the snowman. She clawed at one of its coal-lump eyes, gouging it from its frozen socket. The snowman roared again. Its hold on Violet loosened and Bertie grabbed the little girl from its open mouth, dragging

her out of danger. Then the snowman turned its attention to Lucy, unsheathing icicle claws every bit as ferocious as its teeth. It swiped at her face, but she ducked out of the way just in time, the ice whooshing past her ear.

"Poles! Use your poles!" Bertie shouted.

"Great idea!" Lucy yelled back. She grabbed one of her skiing poles and brandished it like a sword, stabbing the pointy end right in the middle of the snowman's icy chest. It roared even more ferociously.

Lucy pulled out her pole before stabbing it in again. This time the wound struck deeper. Cracks began opening up all over the snowman's body. It looked down at itself in puzzlement. Seconds later, it exploded into miniscule shards of ice that sprayed into the air and rained down on the three children.

They were saved from the snowman, but other dangers could soon arise. There was no time to lose. Lucy hurriedly took the Wish Book from its leather bag. She thought back to how Havoc had made the opening from Grave Hall to the Tower. She didn't know what he had spelled out, but did remember that he had used her tears. Perhaps this particular type of wish only worked with the tears of a child?

She looked over at Violet, who was leaning against Bertie and quietly sobbing. Lucy didn't like to see her hurt and upset, but it could be to their advantage. Lucy eased her skis closer. Then she removed her gloves and touched Violet's face with her bare fingers, wiping the little girl's tears away. "It'll all be over soon, I promise," she said.

Working quickly, afraid that Violet's tears would freeze on her skin, she began spelling out the words *Take us back to Grave Hall*. As her fingers moved across the holes, sparks began to form in mid-air.

"It's working," whispered Bertie.

The sparks fizzled and died.

Lucy glared at Bertie.

"Sorry," he said.

Lucy focused and started from the beginning again. As she touched the last letter the sparks began forming once more. This time the sparks joined together to form a bright slash. The slash widened into a hole.

"Come on, come on, hurry up," Lucy muttered.

As though it had heard her, the hole expanded, and Lucy stared into it, entranced. On the other side she could see the Room of Curiosities, as clear and real as though she was standing inside it.

Behind Lucy, Violet screamed again.

Lucy turned. To her horror, she saw Amethyst standing there holding Violet by the arm and dangling her in mid-air. Havoc Reek was standing behind Bertie, one hand over Bertie's mouth, one arm round his neck.

"Give me the Wish Book and the bottles," Amethyst said, stepping towards Lucy. She stretched out her free hand and clicked her fingers. "Now."

CHAPTER TWENTY-FIVE

THE END FOR LUCY

Lucy stepped away, put the Wish Book and the bag of bottles behind her back.

"No. We're going back to Grave Hall. We know you've been lying. We know what you do to the children you drag here."

"Oh, dearie me," cawed Nevermore.

"Keep that bird quiet or I'll wring its neck," Amethyst snapped. "Lucy. You sweet, idiotic child. I'll explain everything. It's not what it seems. Give me the Wish Book and my bottles. Then we can talk."

"No."

Amethyst sighed. "If you don't, I suppose I'll just have to hurt this one more." She squeezed Violet's arm even tighter and shook her hard, making the little girl scream again.

"Give her the book and the bottles!" Nevermore shrieked, launching herself at Lucy, aiming her claws and beak at Lucy's eyes.

"You want this? You can have it!" Lucy yelled. She swung the Wish Book at Nevermore, catching the tip of her wing. But Nevermore was undeterred. She gave a high-pitched caw before stabbing the back of Lucy's hand with her beak.

The searing pain made Lucy drop the book.

Amethyst released Violet, dropping her into the snow. She stepped over the little girl's huddled, sobbing form towards the Wish Book and Lucy. But just when Lucy thought it was the end for all of them, a familiar rough voice behind her yelled, "Get out of the flipping way!"

Lucy dived away from the opening she'd made.

The very next second something exploded through it and landed on the icy ground.

Huge.

Snarling.

Armed with four sets of scimitar-sharp claws and one set of razor-sharp fangs.

Bathsheba's muscles bunched and rippled beneath her shiny black fur as she moved into a crouch, ready to leap once more. Her roar echoed around the frozen wasteland.

The hoarse voice shouted out again. "Yeah, girl, let's get 'em!" And suddenly Lucy realised who the owner of the mysterious voice was. The voice that she had once thought belonged to a thuggish henchman actually belonged to someone – or something – else altogether. Hunkered down on Bathsheba's back, one and a half ears flattened, orange eye flashing, was Smell.

The two felines flashed past Lucy in a blur of fur and teeth before smashing into Amethyst, who staggered and fell backwards into the snow. With barely a pause, they then sprang at Havoc, who still had Bertie in a headlock. But Bertie twisted free a second before the animals crashed into the magician. Like Amethyst, Havoc stumbled from the force of being hit by a large, wild and angry panther. But he somehow managed to stay upright, although his tricorn hat fell off.

Nevermore tried to flap to safety, but Bathsheba snatched the raven in her jaws. Holding her by one wing, she swung her round several times before suddenly letting her go. Nevermore barrelled through the air, hit a snowdrift at speed and vanished beneath it.

"Lucy! Get yourself and the others through the opening! We'll 'old off this lot till Grave gets 'ere!" yelled Smell as he launched himself from Bathsheba's back. He landed on Havoc's head, crouching there like a bizarre black furry replacement for the hat lying in the snow. The Smell version of a hat enjoyed the added advantage of four sets of claws, which were dug firmly into Havoc's head.

"Aggh!" Havoc yelled, sinking to his knees.

Meanwhile, Bathsheba was keeping herself

occupied with Amethyst, pinning her down, snarling and dripping drool into her face. Amethyst wriggled and squirmed.

Lucy rushed over to Violet and helped her to her feet. One of the little girl's skis had fallen off. Lucy quickly took the other one off too and then her own. Skis would make it hard to climb through the hole.

"Violet, listen. You have to go through that opening," Lucy said urgently.

"But I'm scared. What's on the other side?"

"Somewhere safe, I promise. You know you can trust me, don't you?"

Violet nodded and allowed Lucy to help her through the hole and into the Room of Curiosities.

"Bertie, come on!" Lucy yelled, snatching up the Wish Book.

But Bertie was standing with his back to the opening, staring at Amethyst fighting with Bathsheba, who was at her most fearsome.

"It's going to kill her!" He turned to Lucy. Tears were streaming down his face.

"Who cares?" Lucy yelled. "Remember what she

did to Kathleen, Bertie. What she would have done to Violet and me. And what she's done to you. She stole you from your father and kept you prisoner all this time! She doesn't deserve you caring about her!"

"I can't let it kill her!" Bertie said, and ran to where the others were fighting. And to Lucy's utter despair, he threw himself on top of Bathsheba and began trying to pull her off Amethyst.

By now, Nevermore had dug herself out of the snowdrift. She flew lopsidedly towards Smell. She grabbed his tail in her beak, and yanked at it. Smell yowled and released his grip on Havoc, who swiped the cat off his head and into the snow. Havoc straightened up and staggered towards Lucy. She clutched the Wish Book tighter to her chest.

"I won't let you have it!" she yelled.

Havoc didn't reply. Instead, he ripped open the bag of bottles that Lucy had left lying on the ground, grabbed one of the bottles, yanked the stopper out and poured the contents straight down his throat before dropping the empty bottle. He stared at Lucy and laughed. Then he closed his eyes and threw his hands in the air. Magic crackled at the end of his fingertips.

Several very bad things happened all at once.

The hole Lucy had opened made a sucking noise and vanished.

An invisible force seemed to drag Bathsheba away from Amethyst, tumbling Bertie off the panther. Then Bathsheba whipped through the air and thumped down beside Smell, who seemed unable to move. At the same time, Lucy was propelled through the snow, landing face down at Havoc's boots. He bent over and pulled the Wish Book from her grasp.

Seconds later, four sets of iron bars shot upwards out of the ground. The bars formed a cage round the two animals. Bathsheba roared with rage and leaped at the trap, gnawing ferociously on the metal bars. When she realised she couldn't bite her way through, Bathsheba began scrabbling at the snow around the bottom of the cage. But it was no good. The ground beneath the fluffy layer of snow was so solidly frozen that digging was impossible.

"It works! It really works!" Havoc yelled, sweeping

his arm through the air.

"Excellent work, Havoc," said Amethyst. Her face was very white, and livid red scratches covered her arms. Her fur cloak hung in tatters, shredded by Bathsheba's claws. But her eyes still glittered dangerously.

"What are you going to do to Lucy, Mother? You won't hurt her, will you?" Bertie asked.

"Bertie, my love, she's not worth your concern," Amethyst said, putting her arm round his shoulders. "I made a mistake. This girl is not what she seems. I thought she was a poor vulnerable child whom Grave wanted to exploit. But no. She's working for him. It was all a ruse to find where I was hiding. To get to the children I was sheltering. You saw how she gave poor dear Violet to him without a second thought. She gave him Kathleen too."

"No, Bertie! She's lying! Remember what I told you about Kathleen? About your parents. Your real parents!" Lucy yelled. "And the bottles! How can you believe her now?"

Bertie turned to Lucy, his face twisted in disgust.

"I thought you were my friend. But everything you've told me is a lie. You're a filthy double-crosser. I don't care what happens to you now." With that, he picked up his ski poles and headed for the Tower.

"This is the end for you, Lucy," Amethyst said. She grabbed Lucy's arm and began dragging her back towards the Tower as well. Havoc followed, lugging the Wish Book and the bag of bottles.

"The end, the end, the end," cawed Nevermore as she swooped erratically over their heads.

CHAPTER TWENTY-SIX

SLAMMING THE DOOR

Lucy wriggled, trying hopelessly to loosen the ropes that bound her forearms to the arms of the dungeon chair.

"So we're doing it now?" Havoc said.

"Yes. Now," Amethyst replied. She bent over and pulled the ropes tighter, so that they bit into Lucy's flesh.

"And then what?"

"What we always planned. Attack Grave and

MAAM. Capture them. Take their powers for our own."

"How do we do that?"

"We use a similar technique to the tears. I have it all worked out. And then I can do what I want with no interference."

"We, surely?"

"Yes, Havoc, we, of course. We can cast the magic we want. No one will be able to stop us. We'll show Grave and the rest of MAAM exactly what we're capable of!" Amethyst was ranting now and sounded completely unhinged.

Havoc looked slightly taken aback by Amethyst's wild demeanour. "Shouldn't we wait until we have more bottles before we attack?"

"This girl will give us what we need, all by herself. And I don't want to wait. Grave will find us sooner or later and try to attack. We need to strike first. And there's my boy. I have to protect him."

Lucy finally found her voice and shouted, "He's not your boy! He's Lord Grave's son!"

Amethyst slapped her stingingly hard across the

face. "He's mine, mine, mine. Havoc, stop standing there looking gormless. I need a bottle. Go and fetch one from my study."

As Havoc and Nevermore left the dungeon, despair flooded Lucy. Amethyst was right. This *was* the end. She was going to be made to cry herself to death. Smell and Bathsheba were going to die of cold in the cage Havoc had conjured up. Bertie and Lord Grave would never be reunited. Amethyst would drink enough tears to be able to regain her powers and take down Lord Grave and the rest of MAAM. And who knew what she would do after that?

And Lucy was to blame for it all.

"Oh, Mum, oh, Dad" she cried aloud. She was never going to see them again, or her pet cat Phoebe, or her bedroom at Leafy Ridge.

"*Oh, Mum, oh, Dad*" Amethyst mimicked. "Why are you pining over your pathetic parents?"

"They're not pathetic!"

Amethyst shook her head, as though she was feeling really sorry for Lucy. "Poor deluded child," she said in a more kindly voice. She stared at Lucy, her eyes beginning to glow in the same fiery way they had the night Lucy stole the playing card. Lucy's head began to buzz and ache. Strange thoughts crept and crawled into her brain.

Amethyst's right.

My parents are pathetic.

They would have left me to starve rather than stop gambling.

And they were cruel. I remember that Christmas when I was little. I wanted a wooden train and they somehow managed to get me one. Mum saved up for it. But I didn't even have it for a whole day. They used it as a gambling stake when they ran out of money.

"No! That never happened!" Lucy yelled. "I know what you're trying to do! It won't work with me!"

But more images swirled around in Lucy's mind.

Her parents eating a delicious chicken pie and giving her only the scorched pastry to eat. Laughing at her.

"Not true, not true," Lucy moaned. But the images kept coming and grew worse, as though she was having a waking nightmare.

A nightmare.

She'd learned how to end nightmares, hadn't she?

Lucy summoned up all the mental strength she had left. She imagined a door. A door like the one at Grave Hall. Immensely strong with a gleaming lion's -head knocker. She put the door between herself and the terrible false memories flooding her brain. Then imagined slamming it with all her might, slamming it hard and forever shut.

Amethyst flinched, as though she'd heard the slam.

The dreadful pictures in Lucy's mind vanished.

"How did you do that?" Amethyst said, the fire in her eyes dwindling to sparks.

Lucy said nothing, but concentrated on keeping the door in her mind tightly closed. Little prickles pressed against it like thorns as Amethyst attempted once more to force false thoughts on her. The door shook and the lion's-head knocker rattled. But Lucy's concentration never wavered.

The door held firm.

Amethyst was panting now, as though she'd been

running, and the fire in her eyes had completely died. "You can't keep me out forever. I'll make you see the truth about your parents. Why do you children always love them so much? Why do you all cry out for them? *Mummy, Daddy, Mummy, Daddy*. Makes me sick. But at least it gives me the best, most powerful tears."

Lucy wriggled furiously in her seat, trying to work herself free. "We love our parents because they love us! They try to do their best for us, even when they get it wrong. Not like you! You're a terrible parent!"

Amethyst's eyes began to glow. "How dare you!"

"It's true. You're the worst parent I've ever met!"

"Well, *I* never dragged my Bertie in and out of stinking gambling dens!" Amethyst's nasty smile made her beautiful face ugly.

"My parents made mistakes, but they were still good to me. My dad used to sing me nonsense rhymes to cheer me up when I was ill. He'd scorch me my favourite pie. And my mum would save pennies every week to buy me a birthday present she couldn't really afford. Remind me again, what did you ever do for Bertie?"

Amethyst's smile faded.

"Let's see. You stole him from his father. Lied to him. Kept him cooped up in this tower in the middle of nowhere with nothing to do and no one to be friends with. Then when he did find some friends in the children you kidnapped, they soon vanished from his life again. That's a terrible thing to do! And Bertie will find out the truth sooner or later. Then he'll hate you forever!"

Amethyst's face twisted with rage, even as tears sprang from her eyes. She turned and began banging her fists against the walls. Lucy felt the ground shudder.

Amethyst spun back to face Lucy. "I'll make you suffer. You'll be begging to be bottled by the end. Where is that useless lump of a man? Why hasn't he brought the bottle?" Amethyst stalked out of the dungeon, shrieking Havoc's name.

The tower shook harder.

Lucy desperately tried to pull her arms free from their bindings. Amethyst would be back any moment with a bottle and Lucy had no intention of crying all her love, energy and curiosity into it in order to make Amethyst more powerful. She twisted her wrists this way and that. The rough ropes scraped and burned her skin, but didn't loosen.

"I can't do it!" she half-sobbed in frustration.

"You need to relax, if you can. It'll help. There's an art to untying knots, you know, I read a book on it once," a voice replied.

CHAPTER TWENTY-SEVEN

A HOLE LOT OF TROUBLE

And with that, Bertie was there, working at the ropes, freeing Lucy in seconds.

She leaped out of the chair and then snatched up her fur cloak and the Wish Book from the dungeon floor while Bertie grabbed the bag of bottles. Together they raced out of the dungeon and up the stairs.

"You were pretending to believe Amethyst? You didn't really?" Lucy said breathlessly as they ran.

"I think I almost did at first. It was easier than believing those terrible things about my . . . about her. But then I fell asleep. I had another dream about my mother. My real mother. And I knew it all had to be true."

As Lucy and Bertie reached the ground floor and headed for the entrance hall, the Tower began creaking and groaning. Candles fell from their holders and guttered out. Chips of ceiling began dropping like stony rain, and snow began to drift down through the holes.

"What's happening?" Bertie shouted.

"I don't know!"

They dashed towards the door. They were almost there when the floor began to rumble and shake. The ground beneath their feet split violently apart.

"We'll have to go round it!" Bertie shouted above the crash of falling stone and creaking timbers.

Lucy saw what he meant. There was a narrow ledge of stone left between the walls and the newly formed hole in the floor. The way out lay on the other side. By flattening themselves against the wall and moving on tiptoe, they managed to edge along inch by nerve-wracking inch towards safety, Lucy in front, Bertie behind.

They were almost at the Tower door, when Lucy's foot slipped and suddenly her right leg was dangling over the chasm. She began to tip sideways. As she desperately windmilled her arms, trying to keep her balance, the Wish Book fell from her grasp. It tumbled into the depths below, bouncing and clanging against the sides as it went, pages flying from it. Just as Lucy began to fear she was about to follow, Bertie grabbed her and wrenched her out of danger. Then the two of them hurled themselves through the open Tower door and outside. Lucy fell sprawling on to the icy path. As Bertie helped her to her feet, the Tower behind them began to collapse completely, leaning closer and closer to the ground as it shed bigger and bigger chunks of rock.

"We need to get away from here!" Bertie yelled.

The two of them began to stagger through the snow, which was knee-deep in places.

"If only I'd thought to bring the skis!" Bertie said.

The falling snow was whipping itself into a blizzard

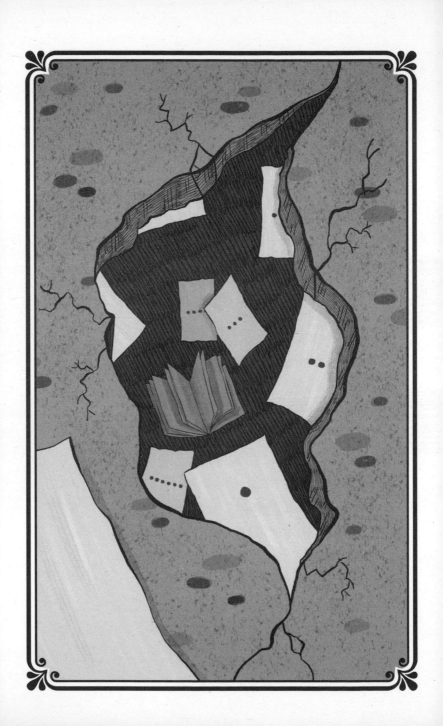

now and Lucy could barely make out Bertie's face, even though he was right beside her. But she could hear the panic in his voice when he yelled: "Wolf!"

A very large and strangely lumpy animal careered towards them through the whirling snowflakes. Because the deep snow made running out of the question, Lucy was about to brace herself for a terrible fight. But then she realised the animal wasn't a wolf after all.

It was Smell and Bathsheba!

Bathsheba bounded up and began butting her head gently against Lucy's stomach. Then she turned her attention to Bertie and began sniffing curiously at him. Bertie took a few steps backwards, his eyes wide with fear.

"It's all right. Bathsheba's on our side." Lucy risked giving the panther a friendly scratch behind the ears. "So is Smell. I thought they'd both be frozen to death by now!"

"Me too," said Smell, who was balanced on Bathsheba's back.

Bertie's expression shifted from alarm to

astonishment. Lucy couldn't blame him. Although she'd got used to the raven and later Nevermore speaking, a talking cat was still something of a shock.

"Why have you never spoken to me before now?" Lucy asked Smell.

"Grave's instructions. Told me to play dumb while keeping my eye on you."

"You *were* spying, weren't you? I knew it!"

"Oi," said Smell. "Not spying. Protecting."

But Lucy merely folded her arms across her chest. "Didn't do a very good job, did you?"

"Don't think now's the time, Lucy," Smell said hastily.

"No. I suppose not. How did you get out of the cage?"

"Dunno. It was there one minute, gone the next."

Lucy remembered what Amethyst had said about some bottles of magic being stronger than others. Havoc must have chosen one of the weaker bottles so the magic had run out quickly. At long last, something was going their way.

"Oh, Smell, the Wish Book's destroyed! How are

we going to get out of here without it? You said before that Lord Grave was on his way?"

Smell twitched his one and a half ears back and forth to rid them of snow. "Er . . . that was just to worry them two criminals, Shade and Reek. Truth is, no one actually knows exactly where we are. Grave will know by now that me and Bathy have disappeared – we were guarding the Room of Curiosities while he was in a meeting. I s'pose there's a chance the magic that book created when you opened the hole might 'ave left a trace. Grave could track that trace to find out where we are. But that sort of caper takes time."

"How much time?"

"A day. P'raps less."

"Amethyst will kill us long before that! Or we'll all freeze to death! Isn't there any magic *you* can do to get us out of here?"

"Me?" Smell said. "I'm a cat, not a magician."

"But you're not *just* a cat? You can talk for a start – that's a bit unusual, isn't it?"

"Too complicated to explain now."

"What about Bathsheba?"

"Bathy? No magic there. She might 'ave a complete set of ears, but there's not that much going on between 'em if you ask me."

Bathsheba growled as though she understood she'd just been grievously insulted.

"So what are we going to do?" said Lucy, hope draining from her.

"Well, there is this one particular magical skill. Involves imagining where you wanna be and then—"

"But that's no good. None of us are magicians!" said Lucy crossly. "Unless . . . Bertie! You're the son of a magician. You must have some magic in you!"

"That's not a very scientific conclusion!" Bertie replied.

"You can review the evidence later! Come on! You need to imagine us back to Grave Hall!"

"'Ang on. Who's the son of a magician? What you talking about?" Smell said.

"I'll explain later, Smell. Come on, Bertie!"

"But I don't remember what Grave Hall looks like!" Bertie said.

"There's a room called the Room of Curiosities.

I'll describe it and you try to imagine it. It's our only hope, Bertie."

Bertie agreed, and they both closed their eyes. Lucy conjured up an image of the Room of Curiosities, trying to remember details of the place where they so desperately needed to be. Then she described those details to Bertie. The pink marble floor. The plinths with their strange objects.

"Lucy, I'm starting to remember it myself! I used to sneak in there when I was little! Some of the curiosities really gave me the creeps!" Bertie cried.

"You remember the Room of Curiosities? 'Ow?" Smell asked.

But neither Lucy nor Bertie stopped to explain, because sparks had begun to appear in the frosty air, forming a bright slash, which widened into a hole. The two children stared in amazement as sure enough, there on the other side of the hole, lay the Room of Curiosities. To Lucy's delight and relief, she could see Mrs Crawley and Lord Grave waiting there.

"Thank goodness you're safe," Lord Grave said. "You must hurry, all of you! Lucy, as the opener of the hole you must go last, otherwise it'll shut as soon as you reach this side."

"But I didn't—"

Lord Grave went rather red in the face. "For once, will you do exactly what I say! You, boy, come through, hurry!"

A shell-shocked Bertie clambered through the opening, then Smell and Bathsheba leaped to safety after him. Lucy slung the bag of bottles over her shoulder and grasped the edges of the opening. It felt soft and rubbery. But at the very last moment, when Lucy was almost in Mrs Crawley's welcoming arms, she was jerked painfully backwards by her hair.

"You're going nowhere!" Lucy heard Amethyst screech.

CHAPTER TWENTY-EIGHT

SEALED

"Take the bag, Mrs Crawley!" Lucy yelled. "Quickly! They mustn't get it!" Mrs Crawley whipped the bag from Lucy's shoulder, which was thankfully a few inches inside the Room of Curiosities.

Amethyst pulled harder at Lucy, who hung on desperately to the edges of the springy hole.

"Shade, let the girl go," Lord Grave commanded, over Lucy's head.

"I'm keeping her. She's something special. You know it too. Why don't you join with us? We could be so powerful together," Amethyst said in a wheedling voice.

"Never," Lord Grave said. "Now do as I say and give me the girl."

"She's mine!" screamed Amethyst, her fingers pulling spitefully and painfully at Lucy's hair.

"Very well. I gave you the chance to end this peacefully." As he spoke, Lord Grave seemed to swell with power and anger. Sparks danced along the edges of his moustache. Then suddenly the sparks launched themselves into the Tower side of the hole, like angry golden insects. Lucy felt their warmth graze her cheek as they zoomed past.

Unfortunately, they bounced straight back out again.

"Duck!" yelled Lord Grave.

Everyone in the Room of Curiosities hastily obeyed.

The sparks hit the wall at the far end of the room and instantly ignited. Lord Grave rapidly muttered some words and the flames died before they could take hold.

Amethyst laughed and dug her sharp fingernails into Lucy's scalp. "You can't do anything, Grave. I spent years protecting this place when I still had power. No human can get through unless I say so. Any magic you try will rebound on you."

"Let the girl go."

"I will. But only if you send my son back through."

"Your son? What are you talking about, woman?"

"I'm not your son!" Bertie shouted. "I don't want anything to do with you."

"You are! You are! I swear it! I'm coming to get you!" Amethyst shrieked.

"Don't be stupid!" Havoc shouted. Although Lucy couldn't see what was happening behind her, Havoc sounded out of breath, as though he'd been running. "You don't have the power to challenge him now! What about our plans?"

"I don't care about any of that! I want him. I want my son!"

The grasp on Lucy's hair suddenly loosened. She

wrenched herself free and tumbled into the Room of Curiosities. She twisted round to see what was happening in the wintry world she had just escaped. She watched as Havoc dragged Amethyst away from the hole. Amethyst, hair hanging over her face, wailed and screamed as she struggled to fight Havoc off and get to her beloved Bertie. Nevermore was there too, flapping around in front of Amethyst's eyes.

"Shall I peck them out, shall I, shall I?" she squawked.

Lord Grave darted forward and helped Lucy to her feet. "You need to close the hole, quickly!"

"Me? But it was Bertie who—"

"Lucy. *You* made the opening. That boy you brought through isn't magical."

Lucy's brain scrambled to understand what this meant. "So I'm a—"

"Yes, a magician. You have been all along. Now you must hurry, imagine the hole closing! As strongly as you can."

Lucy shut her eyes. Imagined the edges of the opening reaching towards each other, getting closer and closer together. A huge gust of wind whipped through the Room of Curiosities, ruffling Lucy's hair. She opened her eyes again just in time to see the hole seal itself shut, leaving Amethyst, Havoc and Nevermore trapped in the barren, frozen wasteland with only a pile of collapsed rubble to shelter them.

CHAPTER TWENTY-NINE

THE EYEBROWS HAVE IT

Lucy found herself engulfed in arms and a beard.
"It's all right, it's all right, you're safe now,"
Mrs Crawley said in a choked voice, stroking
Lucy's hair. Lucy was happy to stay there for
a while, waiting for her heart to slow and her legs to
stop shaking. She might also have secretly shed a
tear or two of relief.

When Lucy finally emerged from the cook's
comforting embrace, she saw Lord Grave staring

dumbstruck at Bertie.

"You look just like . . . is it . . . could you be . . .?"

"Please open this, sir. I think it'll prove everything," Bertie said, his voice trembling. He handed his velvet pouch to Lord Grave.

Lord Grave touched the velvet gently, but didn't open it. "I don't need proof. I'd know you anywhere. You're my Albert!"

"Well, wet my whiskers! 'As to be, I s'pose, with them eyebrows," said Smell.

Lord Grave guffawed and then hugged Bertie. He didn't let him go for a long time. When he finally did, his eyes were wet.

Lucy smiled to see them together, but at that moment, more than anything else in the world, all she wanted was to feel her own parents' arms round her.

Lord Grave took out a handkerchief and wiped his eyes. Then he stepped towards Lucy as though he wanted to hug her too, but wasn't quite sure how to go about it. In the end, he settled for shaking her hand up and down very vigorously.

"Well done, Lucy, well done. We thought we'd lost you," he said.

"Where's Violet?" Lucy suddenly panicked because she couldn't see the little scullery maid.

"Calm yourself. Vonk is taking care of her. We know her memory has been tampered with, but we can deal with that. She's come to no real harm, thanks to you."

"I'm so sorry," Lucy said, touching Lord Grave's sleeve. "I'm sorry I stole the Wish Book and caused all this trouble. Havoc lied to me about everything. I shouldn't have been so quick to believe him."

"It's not your fault. It's mine. Taking you away from your parents like that, with no explanation, was a serious error on my part."

"I blooming told you so," Smell said.

"But why *did* you take me away?" asked Lucy.

"I used to be head of an organisation called MAAM. Which stands for—

"Magicians Against the Abuse of Magic?" Lucy said.

Lord Grave raised his eyebrows in surprise.

"Correct. I retired when Albert was stolen as I no longer had the heart for the job. But when I heard about a young girl winning an unusual number of poker games, I suspected misuse of magic. All my old MAAM instincts kicked in, so I investigated. When I met you, I realised you had no idea how powerful you were. You needed guidance to develop your talents in the proper manner. That's why I brought you here."

"Why didn't you tell me all this from the start?"

"I wanted to discover what sort of person you were first. To be sure of you before I let you learn of your gifts. After all, you were abusing magic for financial gain, which is a very serious crime."

Lucy blushed. "Sorry. I had to though . . ."

Lord Grave waved his hand dismissively. "No need to explain. We've both made mistakes. Now, you must all be very hungry. Let's have some breakfast."

After breakfast (which was served by a mystified and extra grumpy Becky Bone, who deliberately dropped the milk jug in Lucy's lap), Bertie and Lucy went with

Lord Grave, Mrs Crawley and Smell into the drawing room where Bertie stood and stared for a long time at the portrait of him and his mother.

"If only she was still alive," he said wistfully.

Lord Grave put his hand on Bertie's shoulder. "You know, you kept that teething ring with you all the time after she died, refused to let it go. So I had a pouch and cord made for it so you could wear it round your neck. You were wearing it when you vanished from your bed that night."

"Stolen, you mean. By Amethyst?" Bertie asked.

"I actually always rather suspected Havoc Reek did it at Amethyst Shade's request. Although I couldn't know for sure. To the outside world, I pretended you were dead. But I never stopped trying to find you. Now, let's sit down."

When everyone was settled on the various drawing-room sofas, Smell padded over to Lucy and jumped up on to her knee.

"Wish I'd been able to stop that blackguard Reek nicking you in the first place," he said, looking up at her.

"Another mistake. I should have known he'd get distracted by food or fall asleep on the job. It's not the first time it's happened," Lord Grave said.

Smell didn't reply. He seemed to have decided it was vitally important at that precise moment to wash his tail.

"So, what about Amethyst, sir, who is she really? Why did she end up at that tower?" Bertie asked.

"It's a long story, my boy. The short version is that Amethyst Shade and Havoc Reek began dabbling in a forbidden branch of magic. One which involves harnessing the power of children. We stopped them. Took their powers away. Or at least, we thought we had. Shade managed to retain just enough power to escape. No one could find her. Now we know why. She was hidden in some remote part of the world. She must have created her refuge there before we took her powers."

"And what about Havoc?" Lucy asked.

"We did the job properly with him. Caught and imprisoned him in the Room of Curiosities. We could have killed him instead, but I thought he might one day lead me back to Bertie."

"Did you know Amethyst was the one stealing children?" Lucy asked.

"We suspected as much; that she must be out there somewhere, experimenting with the power of children," Lord Grave said. "But she was always one step ahead of us."

"You were right," Lucy said. She explained how Amethyst had been bottling children's tears, planning to use their power to take on Lord Grave and MAAM again. Then she looked through the bag of bottles until she found a half-full one.

"These are Kathleen's tears, I think. She was a friend of ours," Lucy said, holding it up.

Lord Grave took the bottle from her and stared at it thoughtfully.

"She was so kind," Lucy added, remembering Kathleen finding clothes for her. How she'd looked after Violet and comforted her when she'd been upset. Perhaps Lord Grave would be able to bring Kathleen back? How wonderful that would be. She imagined Kathleen with them in the drawing room, alive and well and happy.

There was the sound of breaking glass. Lucy opened her eyes. She hadn't even realised they were closed. To her amazement, the bottle in Lord Grave's hand had exploded into shards of blue. Everyone watched, transfixed, as the shards swirled around the room before beginning to change colour and form themselves into a flesh-and-blood girl, who turned slowly in mid-air, before gently dropping on to the thick rug.

Bertie ran to Kathleen and knelt beside her.

"Where are we, Bertie? What happened to me?" Kathleen looked around, dazed.

"It's all right. Don't worry, we're safe here," Bertie said, hugging Kathleen.

"Mrs Crawley, take the girl to the kitchen, give her some hot sweet tea," Lord Grave said, as Bertie helped Kathleen stand. The two of them followed Mrs Crawley out of the room, Bertie turning and smiling gratefully at Lucy.

"Would you be able to do the same to the rest of them?" Lucy asked, when she'd recovered a little

from the shock of seeing Kathleen unbottled.

"We can give it a try. Let's get them out of their bag. Line them up on the table here," Lord Grave said, and began clearing papers off a table that stood in the bay window of the drawing room. When they'd put the last bottle out, Lord Grave said, "Well, come along, Lucy, it's over to you now."

"Me? Why?"

"I didn't liberate your friend from that bottle just now. *You* did that."

"Are you really sure?"

"Think about all the other things you've done. You used the playing card, for one. Only a magician would be able to do that. You trapped Turner and Paige by controlling the magical door that guards the reading room. And of course, the Wish Book responded to your command."

"But only the very first time, and that was with Havoc telling me what to do. And the second time I used Violet's tears to make the book work."

"It was all you Lucy, Reek may have needed the power of tears, but *you* didn't. And what you did just now, the way you freed that girl . . ." Lord Grave shook his head. "Even I'm not sure what magic was involved there."

"But all I was doing was thinking about what a nice person she was and all the kind things she'd done."

"Fascinating," Lord Grave said. "Most unusual. I think we should use the same method for the rest of the bottles. If we work together, I'm sure we can do it."

"But I don't know any of these children or even what they look like."

"Wait a minute," said Lord Grave. He went over to a desk on the other side of the room. He rummaged around and brought a small pile of newspaper cuttings back with him.

"The *Penny* is a frightful old rag, but it did tirelessly report the children who've gone missing over the last few years." He spread the cuttings out on the table. Each had a drawing of a missing child printed on it.

"Does that help, Lucy?"

"I think so. Maybe if we imagine them here in this room with us?"

Lucy sat next to Lord Grave and studied all the pictures of the missing children, fixing their faces in her mind. She imagined them in Lord Grave's drawing room with them, chatting and laughing.

The bottles began to shudder. Then, like Kathleen's bottle, they exploded, the glass flying right up to the ceiling. The shards hovered, tinkling gently, before separating into groups. The groups began to spin, the shards forming into outlines of girls and boys, which quickly became flesh-and-blood children. One by one they dropped gently to the drawing-room floor. The last to land was a short, thin boy with untidy hair and a mole on his left cheek.

"Where am I?" said Eddie Robinson. Then he stared at Lucy, "And why are you wearing my shirt?"

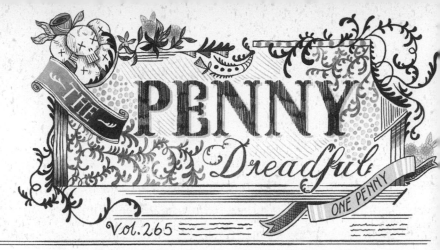

THE PENNY Dreadful

ONE PENNY

Vol. 265

MISSING CHILDREN FOUND!

THE *PENNY* is delighted to inform its readers that the majority of the children who have gone missing over the last year have been found alive and well.

According to a source at Grave Hall, Lord Grave was involved in the discovery and rescue of the missing children, who were found enslaved in a clandestine long-john factory in the wilds of Antarctica. Tragically, however, not all of the missing children have been recovered and it is thought some did not survive the icy conditions. But no zombies were involved.

CHAPTER THIRTY

GOODLY AND GRAVE

Over the next few days, the bottled children were reunited with their parents. They all had their memories tweaked (as Lord Grave called it) before leaving Grave Hall, so that they really did believe they'd been trapped in a freezing long-john factory the whole time, weaving woollen undergarments for no pay.

"But why do you need to tweak their memories? Why not let people know the truth?" Lucy had asked.

"We prefer to keep magic hidden from non-magicians as much as possible. They wouldn't understand. It would frighten them. That's why most of the staff here are magical."

"But not Violet and Becky?"

"They're the only ones who aren't. Violet works part-time and doesn't live here, so it's reasonably easy to keep things secret from her." Lord Grave coughed. "As for Becky . . . well, she is the most unobservant non-magical person I have ever encountered. She wouldn't notice magic if it wrote her a letter introducing itself."

Kathleen was the last of the bottled children to go home. After watching her being collected by her ecstatic parents, Lucy wandered down to the kitchen. Bathsheba's suppertime was near.

"Are you all right?" Mrs Crawley asked Lucy as she filled Bathsheba's bucket with the usual raw, dripping meat.

Lucy nodded, avoiding Mrs Crawley's eyes.

"I'm sure they'll be in touch soon," Mrs Crawley said.

Lucy had written to Mr and Mrs Goodly a few days ago to let them know that Lord Grave was letting her go home. But she had heard nothing back from them yet, so she didn't know if her letter had even reached them. What if something had happened to them both? Without her around, they could have ended up in all sorts of trouble.

Lucy knew that if Mrs Crawley saw she was upset, she'd try to be kind. Lucy wouldn't be able to bear that. So she kept her head down, grabbed the bucket and began lugging it towards the wildlife enclosure. Unfortunately, she encountered Becky in the kitchen garden, who was pulling up vegetables for Mrs Crawley.

"No more cosy breakfasts with his Lordship, then? Back to being a boot girl? Is that why you're so down in the mouth, Goodly?" Becky said gleefully, jabbing Lucy's arm with a carrot.

Lucy ignored her and carried on walking. At least she was only feeding Bathsheba this evening and not cleaning out her hut, so there was no need to put on her armour and go into the wildlife park.

When Lucy reached the iron fence, she dejectedly climbed a ladder that leaned against it. When she reached the top of the ladder, Lucy tipped the meat out of the bucket over into the animals' side. The smell of food soon brought Bathsheba bounding up. As the panther tore hungrily at her grisly meal, Lucy stayed on the ladder and looked out across the grounds of Grave Hall. The sun was beginning to set. Down by the lake, the elephants were playing an evening water game. Lord Grave had told her one of the elephants was due to have a baby soon. Lucy wondered if she would still be here then?

As she sat there, trying to tell herself everything would be fine in the end, she saw two people walking slowly up the long drive towards the house. One of the figures looked like it had three legs.

Lucy frowned. How puzzling. Maybe it was a trick of the light?

No, not three legs.

Two legs and a walking stick!

Lucy stood up on the top rung of the ladder, waved and shouted and nearly toppled into Bathsheba's enclosure. Bathsheba roared in surprise at Lucy's antics and jumped up at the fence. But, unlike the excited panther, the two figures didn't hear Lucy. They kept making their slow, steady way towards Grave Hall.

Lucy scrambled down the ladder and began to run faster than she'd ever run before. The gravel crunched beneath her boots as she flew down the drive, half laughing, half sobbing.

And then there they were in front of her, shadowy in the last of the sun's red rays, arms outstretched. She hurled herself into their hugs and kisses, her mother sobbing and her father burying his face in her hair, saying over and over again, "My girl, my girl, oh my dear, dear girl."

Lucy closed her eyes, so very thankful to be reunited with her family at last. She hugged them and hugged them, then hugged them some more. But after a while she became aware of a very strange smell. She looked around. It couldn't be Smell smelling as there was no sign of him. And anyway, the smell didn't smell like Smell. It was more of a smoky aroma, as though someone was burning wood.

Lucy gave her parents a last squeeze and then stood back, with her hands on her hips. Her mother's hair was all frazzled at the ends and her cheek was smeared with soot.

"What happened?" Lucy asked.

"Oh dear," said Mrs Goodly, her voice trembling.

"So unfortunate," said Mr Goodly, shaking his head.

"Meow," said the basket Mrs Goodly was clutching.

"Is Phoebe in that basket? Why have you brought her here? Why isn't she at Leafy Ridge? You haven't gambled our house away, have you?" Lucy said, her voice getting louder.

"Certainly not!" said Mr Goodly, looking most offended.

"We went into the village for a quick game of bridge. They have a club, you know," Mrs Goodly began. "Your father had a pigeon pie in the oven for tea. We were only meant to be gone an hour. But we hit a winning streak. A brief one. Lost track of time.

The pigeon pie caught fire."

"You burned down Leafy Ridge?" Lucy was whispering now because all the shout had gone out of her. "What are we going to do? Where will we live?"

Mr and Mrs Goodly hung their heads and didn't reply.

"Ah, Mr and Mrs Goodly! How wonderful to see you again!" Lord Grave boomed from behind Lucy. He and Bertie were striding down the drive towards them.

"I hear you've had a slight mishap," Lord Grave said when he reached them. He puffed on the cigar he was smoking. "Not to worry, not to worry. Lots of room here at Grave Hall, for tonight at least. Do come inside. Mrs Crawley will no doubt be able to conjure up some supper."

Mrs Goodly said, "Oh, no, thank you. Now you've kindly given us our Lucy back again, we can get going and work on rebuilding our fortune."

"I see. As long as it's what Lucy wants too?"

"Are you really going to leave us, Lucy?" Bertie said, sounding very disappointed.

"Y-yes, I want to be with my family," Lucy said, hesitating as she said it. Up until a few minutes ago, this *had* been what she wanted. She loved her parents, useless as they were. And they *needed* her. She still had the magical playing card hidden in her bedside table, so she would be able to rebuild the Goodly fortune, staying up all night, working the gambling dens, sleeping all day . . .

Suddenly it didn't sound so appealing. And she'd miss Grave Hall and everyone in it. Most of all, she suddenly realised how desperate she was to learn more about her magical abilities and the magical world. Wasn't that why Lord Grave had taken her from her parents in the first place? Maybe he'd lost interest in teaching her because she'd been so troublesome.

She looked over at Lord Grave, who was eyeing her intently. "I have a proposition," he said.

Lucy's heart gave a little leap of hope.

"Lucy is a very good boot girl. The best I have had the pleasure to employ. If you could spare her for a little longer, I would be most grateful."

Lord Grave spread his arms and touched both the Goodlys on the shoulder. Sparks fizzled under his fingers. Lucy saw them, but her parents didn't. They both smiled at Lord Grave as though he'd given them a sure-fire racing tip.

"Well, that seems reasonable," said Mr Goodly cheerfully.

"But only for a few weeks," said Mrs Goodly.

"Of course. I feel sure in the meantime Lady Luck will be kind to you," said Lord Grave, winking at Lucy.

And so, Mr and Mrs Goodly left Grave Hall to rebuild their fortune. Lucy stood at the front door with Lord Grave, waving them off.

"They don't mean to be so useless. It's just how they are," she said as her parents ambled away. "Will Lady Luck really be kind to them?"

Lord Grave cleared his throat. "Let's just say, if I was a gambling man myself, I'd put a bet on it. You don't need to worry about them."

"Am I really the best boot girl you've ever employed?"

"No. You're absolutely the worst ever. Rude. Rebellious. And you never quite get all the mud out of the seams of my shoes."

Lucy decided not to be offended at Lord Grave's lack of faith in her boot girl skills. "So why *do* you want me to stay?"

"MAAM has been trying to persuade me back for a long time. I've finally agreed to take up the reins again. And I'd like to have you at my side."

"Me?" said Lucy, eyes growing wide.

"Of course. You need help to hone and control your powers, of course, but you have great potential. We could be quite a team. Goodly and Grave. Has quite a ring to it, don't you think?" Lord Grave said.

"I could help too!" Bertie piped up.

"I thought you said you didn't believe in magic?" Lucy replied.

"I don't. I still think it can all be explained by science." Bertie cast an anxious look at his father. "But I could provide practical advice to you both."

Lord Grave smiled and ruffled Bertie's hair. "Why not? Let's call it an advisory role."

The three of them turned and made their way inside. Vonk and Mrs Crawley were in the entrance hall, waiting to meet them.

"Very glad you've decided to stay, Lucy," said Vonk. "Any chance of having my shears back?"

"Oh, I think I might have left them behind at the Tower. Sorry," Lucy said, feeling rather guilty.

Vonk winked. "Only joking. Good to have you back, Lucy."

"Come along, everyone. I'm going to serve you all a very special celebration dinner. A new recipe in Lucy's honour!" Mrs Crawley declared.

Lucy stifled a groan. "That'll be lovely, thanks very much."

"You're very welcome. By the way, what's in that basket?"

"Oh, poor Phoebe! They forgot to take her with them!" Lucy said and ran back down the drive to fetch the basket, which had been sitting there all this time. She opened it up and Phoebe leaped out with an indignant meow before trotting into the entrance hall where she gave Lord Grave and the rest of the household a quick sniff each. Then she padded curiously over to the grand, sweeping staircase. She stopped, one paw on the bottom step. Her tail bristled. The next moment, Smell came bounding down the stairs towards her. His orange eye was even rounder and bulgier than ever.

"Well, *hello*!" he said. "Things are certainly looking up round 'ere!"

THE END

Acknowledgements

Huge thanks to...

My agent, Kate Shaw. I couldn't have done this without you, Kate! My wonderful editors Ruth Alltimes and Harriet Wilson for their patient and brilliant advice and the rest of the fantastic team at HarperCollins *Children's Books*. Becka Moor for her fabulous illustrations. Nikki for being so supportive and enthusiastic, and Rhod, too, for encouraging me. Ann and Tony Ward for being such great friends. All my writer friends, especially those from the Writing Asylum.

Finally, the biggest thanks of all go to my husband for always believing in me.